Selected as an *Observer* essential summer read
Selected as one of *Parade*'s Best Books of Au
Selected as one of BookBub's Must
Literary Fiction of A
Selected as one of B
Sally

'Kate Weinberg writes with ... copying bits to show people. ... ong With Her is so beautifully perceptiv ... isically observed; she writes about the complexities of human relationships in a way that stops me in my tracks' Jojo Moyes

'A hallucinatory, amazingly capacious novel ... It's a testament to Weinberg's writing that I wouldn't have minded staying in her feverish world for longer' *Daily Telegraph*

'It's so beautiful. And so painful. And so gorgeously descriptive of a devastating chapter that so many of us just don't know or understand even, with all compassion' Sarah Jessica Parker

'I was cheered by the warmth of friends and by the hard-won compassion, even optimism ... *There's Nothing Wrong With Her* is full of surprises' *Financial Times*

'Surreal, magical and totally original, this beautiful novel provides a powerful insight into a world and experience that science is struggling to explain or navigate. Luminous' Sathnam Sanghera

'A funny, philosophical novel that perfectly captures the surreal state of invisible illness ... Remarkable ... As funny as it is moving ... A book about life' independent.co.uk

'Such a thoughtful exploration of the traps of grief and chronic illness. Beautifully conjured, with shades of *The Yellow Wallpaper*, but brilliantly modernised' Sara Collins

'Funny and painfully true. A book of revelations. This is a beautiful capture of what it means to live with a chronic illness. The best thing you'll read this year' Kiley Reid

'A really wonderful piece of work: so fresh. It encompasses so many things: a whole life – sorrows, damage, hopes' Richard Curtis

'I felt like I was right there in her bedroom with Vita, day after day, seeing the visions, feeling the pain, struggling to make sense of it all ... An important novel about invisible illnesses. Go read it right now, like literally right now' Betches

'Darkly funny' *Katie Couric Media*

'This fresh, authentic novel stops you in your tracks and makes you reflect on life. As you become deeply invested in Vita's road to recovery, you may find yourself considering what's holding you back from being the fullest, messiest, most alive version of yourself, too. A smart, significant read' *Heat*

'Slim in size but vast in emotional impact, Kate Weinberg's novel explores the landscape of one woman's life – her heart, her family, her pain and her desires. A work of dazzling bravery' Jenny Jackson

'Delicious … A witty tale of panic, lust and the search for identity' Jason Isaacs

'I sped through it. It's deep and dark and beautiful' Esther Freud

'An original and enchanting read' *Strong Words*

'A compelling commentary on mental health' *Woman & Home*

'I've never read anything like it. A brilliant mass of contradictions … It's light and dark, funny and moving, soulful and sexy, quirky and important. A delight and an education on every page' Emma Freud

'Long Covid is not the obvious subject for a quirky almost-romcom but Kate Weinberg pulls it off triumphantly. Touching, funny, inventive, *There's Nothing Wrong With Her* is a beguiling story about illness and faith and the power of love in all its forms. I devoured it in a single greedy sitting' Clare Clark

'An inventive, witty and questioning novel' *Saga*

'A tender, curious and undeniably urgent exploration of the many modern challenges to women's health and happiness. As compassionate as it is incisive, Weinberg's latest makes a persuasive case for the saving graces of our imaginative inner worlds' M L Rio

'This painfully funny novel sizzles with love and desire, isolation and loss, and the incongruous breakthroughs that take place when one has little left to lose' Elizabeth McKenzie

'This novel may delve into The Pit (of ill health, of grief, of despair), but it never feels less than buoyant. Weinberg has found a way to write about chronic illness and pain with great wit, creativity and verve. I loved every page of this short novel and hated to leave its vibrant characters behind' Laura Sims

'Gloriously original, funny and frighteningly observant, reading Kate Weinberg's *There's Nothing Wrong With Her* is like reading your brain turned inside out and seeing all the chaos that goes inside, as written by an author with an astuteness and clarity of voice that is captivating and entirely brilliant. I loved it!' Ore Agbaje-Williams

'*There's Nothing Wrong With Her* is the rarest of reads: unflinchingly honest, wryly funny, and incredibly tender in the moments between. Vita and her eccentric crew are companions we could all use on our toughest days' Leanne Toshiko Simpson

'I couldn't put down this quick, clever novel … Both comic and heart-breaking in equal measure, *There's Nothing Wrong With Her* is a post-pandemic must-read. I'll be thinking about its vivid cast of characters for a good long time' Amy Shearn

'Kate Weinberg has written a gorgeous, engrossing and urgent book. Her unforgettable characters wrestle with a monster that stalks so many lives. Read this for the ones you love who have fought the same long fight' Kevin Sullivan

KATE WEINBERG was born and lives in London. She studied English at Oxford and creative writing in East Anglia. She has worked as a slush pile reader, a bookshop assistant, a journalist and a ghost writer. She is the author of one previous novel, *The Truants.*

kateweinbergwriter.com

There's Nothing Wrong With Her

KATE WEINBERG

BLOOMSBURY PUBLISHING
LONDON • OXFORD • NEW YORK • NEW DELHI • SYDNEY

BLOOMSBURY PUBLISHING
Bloomsbury Publishing Plc
50 Bedford Square, London, WC1B 3DP, UK
Bloomsbury Publishing Ireland Limited,
29 Earlsfort Terrace, Dublin 2, D02 AY28, Ireland

BLOOMSBURY, BLOOMSBURY PUBLISHING and the Diana logo
are trademarks of Bloomsbury Publishing Plc

First published in Great Britain 2024
This edition published 2025

A catalogue record for this book is available from the British Library

ISBN: HB: 978-1-5266-0733-1; TPB: 978-1-5266-8193-5; PB: 978-1-5266-0734-8;
EBOOK: 978-1-5266-0735-5; EPDF: 978-1-5266-6694-9

2 4 6 8 10 9 7 5 3 1

Typeset by Integra Software Services Pvt. Ltd.
Printed and bound in Great Britain by Clays Ltd, Elcograf S.p.A.

MIX
Paper | Supporting responsible forestry
FSC www.fsc.org FSC® C018072

To find out more about our authors and books visit www.bloomsbury.com
and sign up for our newsletters
For product safety related questions contact productsafety@bloomsbury.com

For James, who makes it all better

1

A Visitor

Let's start with some facts.

On Day 126, I moved Whitney Houston up to the end of my bed.

Hold on. Even that's not quite true.

On Day 126, I asked *Max* to move the bowl, filled with water, multi-coloured gravel, plastic coral, treasure chest, ruined archway and Whitney Houston herself, swimming in panicked circles, and bring it sloshing up the nine steps to the mezzanine where he placed it at the end of our bed.

Partly the goldfish-move was for company, a cellmate of sorts. I had only moved into Max's basement flat a couple of weeks before I got sick. So I'd barely unpacked before I began to spend long stretches of the day in bed alone. Max's hours at the hospital were relentless and for weeks now I'd stopped wanting visitors.

But the main idea for having Whitney Houston join me upstairs was that when I feel myself getting sucked back into The Pit it would stop me thinking: *Something truly catastrophic is happening; the doctors won't tell me, but they think I'm stuck like this forever.* Or rather, when I did think that I'd catch sight of my golden fantail, swimming blithely around her bowl, and try to remember that this is how it always feels. The fact that I kept forgetting, this violent yoyo-ing between thinking I was fine and thinking I was stuck forever; this odd, etch-a-sketch memory: well, that was part of the sickness too.

Sometimes it worked, sort of. When I felt the clamp tightening at the back of my skull, when I lost feeling in my fingers and toes and the strange, poisoned aches began to flood my system, I'd fix my gaze on Whitney's translucent tail wafting through the water and remind myself that this panic, this sense of doom that kept circling my brain like a fish in a bowl: that was just the illness speaking.

Mostly it didn't work.

Because the dirty secret was that although I joked about seven-second memories and Jewish hypochondria, this whole episode had dragged on way too long to be funny. By now, everyone was frightened. My friends were frightened, my family was frightened. Even my boss sent orchids in an expensive ceramic pot.

I saw it in Max's eyes too. At least I thought I did. And when a doctor is frightened, you know you better start worrying.

That's the problem with this story, so much of it is guesswork. There aren't enough hard facts. In the end, I did break free, even if I'm still trying to piece together from what. All I knew then was that I had to serve my time, imprisoned by whatever sickness it was. Only thing was, no one would tell me for how long. As the weeks gave way to months, so much else blurred.

Some days, it felt like only Whitney Houston was really there.

The vortex pulls me down and I thrash around inside a wave of pain. Muscles I didn't know exist are crawling with fire. A belt is tightening around my chest. There isn't enough space for my lungs. My brain balls itself up like a frightened bug and everything goes very slow and quiet, like my senses have been plugged. I'm gripped by a powerful loneliness, such a sharp need to touch, hear, or feel the presence of someone else that I'm scared I will not be able to breathe again without it.

Please…

Max.

Gracie.

Anyone.

When I surface, gasping for air, Luigi da Porto is sitting at the end of my bed. Lately he's been stalking my night thoughts. I haven't been able to work out quite why, after all these years, but now that he's here it feels strangely natural. Like when the chronology is skewed in a dream and a dead relative or a teacher from your primary school shows up. I don't think: *Impossible, sixteenth-century Italian warrior–poet Luigi da Porto pitching up in my basement flat in north-west London.* I just think, *Thank God, there he is.*

And just as I think this, his outline begins to blur.

I try to focus on his features, try to get purchase on something solid outside my body, but the next wave from The Pit is crashing over me. This time it brings with it a deadening exhaustion that is almost sweet. I slip back into unconsciousness without a fight.

When I wake again, the mezzanine of our apartment seems brighter than usual. Sun is pouring through the half of the window that's above pavement level, bouncing off Whitney's bowl and Max's favourite painting, which I've been forced to spend rather too much time with: a pair of lovers on London Bridge, standing stock still and lost in each other, as commuters swirl around them.

This time I can see Luigi very clearly. He's lounging on the yellow armchair that Max brought up to our bedroom space for visitors, wearing the same clothes as he was in that oil painting where I first saw and fell for him: a fur-trimmed tunic (cinched rather tight), pantyhose, slip-on leather shoes, and a velvet cloak flicked over one shoulder.

When he sees I'm awake, he leans forward. His broken nose, the thick dark eyebrows, the hollow cheeks and startling fullness of his lips – all the thuggish beauty of his broad features rearranges itself into a picture of concern.

'Oh, my dear, you *are* having an awful time of it, aren't you?'

The clock by Whitney's bowl, the one you can't always trust, says 2.36. I must have been down there for a while this time. Two hours, maybe three? The thought of someone watching me while I am thrashing around in The Pit gives me vertigo. I wipe my mouth quickly with the back of my hand to check for dribble.

'How did you get here?' I try to stack the pillows behind me so I can sit up straight but the effort is too much.

'Can I help with that?' Luigi asks, half-rising. 'I can't tell you how much I feel for you. You know, of course, I was bedridden for several months following the injury. So you don't need to explain to me the *crushing* effect it has on the spirit as well as the body.'

I feel a flicker of guilt. It's true, he's been on my mind. But not because I've been reflecting compassionately on his time stuck in bed. Rather, I've been dreaming lately about my life in Verona, that tiny flat a stone's throw from the Arena stadium, so that in the summer months when the opera was in full swing you didn't need to buy tickets, the music came floating over the rooftops. Wondering when it was that I gave up on that younger part of me: sex on a train, on a boat, and once – a fail – up a tree; the me that believed in poetry (even my own) and got stoned, so very stoned, then pinched warm pastries from the trays outside the bakeries on the way home at 3 a.m; the me that I feel so fucking far from now.

'Mind you,' he lowers his voice, 'I probably shouldn't say this with you feeling so reduced… but you do know your cheekbones have *never* looked better?'

'Oh.' I touch my face, pleased. 'Well, thank you. Someone said I was looking gaunt.'

It seems disloyal to name Max.

'Nonsense. You look ravishing. Even with the strange bed garments. All edges, angles, and pools of dark eyes. If my heart were not already spoken for…'

I glance down at my flimsy grey t-shirt – a favourite, bought in a hipster store in Brooklyn years ago, worn thin with age, now stuck to my back with cold sweat – and a pair of faded black drawstring trousers I've been wearing since yesterday morning. Was that really only yesterday?

Time has collapsed since I got sick. Night and day have lost their seam. Or perhaps that happened a few weeks after, when I realised I wasn't getting any better and the world had moved on without me? Leaving me trapped in this purgatory, a place in which I wake with dread to see which version of myself I will be: a well person who is stalked by sickness, or a sick person who may never get well. The repetition and the solitude are enough to drive you crazy, but seeing people is worse. So you sit with your goldfish and your memories and your boredom and you wait, and wait, and wait.

'How long have you been here?'

'Oh, only a couple of hours. I wasn't bored at all,' says Luigi, waving a hand airily. 'Quite the contrary. I was transported by the most exquisite music coming from upstairs.' He closes his eyes. 'The flow of arpeggios…' his hand traces languid curves in the air '… that haunting melody buried in between.'

I nod carefully. Every muscle in me feels stiff, like I've been pummelled in a boxing match. 'Our upstairs neighbour is a piano teacher. Her students come and go throughout the day.'

'How marvellous,' says Luigi, clapping his hands together. 'What a salve that must be. The sound of angels transporting you from your sickbed.'

'If only. Most of the time it's just scales. Played over and over, badly.'

'Ah, yes. *Torture*. Nothing worse than a stumbling scale. But this was a thing of… startling beauty.'

'Probably the teacher playing then.'

'Flawless for a few minutes.' His nostrils flare, moved by the memory. 'That simple, sad melody arching into that first cadenza, then suddenly—' He breaks off, switches his gaze back to me. 'She is very sad, is she not?'

'Who?'

'The piano teacher.'

'Oh. I don't know actually. Haven't met her yet. I got sick soon after I moved into this flat so…'

'A profound sadness in her tonality. Heartbreak, I'll wager. It takes one to know one—' His face twists suddenly, one side of his mouth disappearing. For a horrible moment I think he is going to burst into tears about… what was her name, the woman who jilted him after his injury? *Lucina Savorgnan.* How could I forget; the betrayal that inspired the greatest love story of all? Then he shakes his head, his expression clearing. 'Ignore me, *cara mia*! I have left all that behind me. I'm here to talk about *you*.' A smile takes over his face again. 'How has life treated you since Verona? Apart from this horrible sickness, of course. You make talking stories, I gather?'

'Talking…? Oh, yes, sort of. I produce this regular podcast—'

'How *thrilling*. Please tell me you are still attached to that wonderful artist who makes worlds?'

It takes me a moment. I'd never thought about him like that. Danny Cousins was an occasional assistant set designer for theatre and opera, who I'd met and fallen hard for in my mid-twenties. He was the reason I went to Verona; I'd followed him out there while he worked for an opera season, leaving behind my lowly job at a publishing imprint for art books and the lovely but not-quite-it boyfriend I'd been seeing. I had a vague notion that I might find something to write about, a book or a screenplay, either way an excuse to stick around and pay my way until Danny's contract ended. But as I dug into Luigi's life, the project that started out as an alibi became an obsession. Soon I was persuading Danny to use a Saturday to explore some new location – the ruins of a villa, the remnants of a ballroom, a river between fields that had once been a battleground – while piecing together Luigi's story.

'Oh. God, no,' I say. 'That ended years ago. I'm with a doctor now.' I gesture at Max's side of the bed, which is much tidier than mine: a radio alarm I've told him is broken (I took the batteries out; on top of a crushing illness, the state of the world is too depressing); two books about climbing; and a bunch of the little clay figures he makes when he has insomnia: a fox, an oak tree with miniature leaves, a motorbike.

'A doctor?' says Luigi, crestfallen. 'What a shame.'

I frown. 'Why would you say that?'

'Dangerous people. Lack nuance.' He shudders. 'When I think of all those instruments of torture they made me wear when I was paralysed…'

'How awful. But that was quite a different time—'

'The whole thing…' He flutters his hands. 'Downright Mediaeval. The truth is what I really needed, over and above someone who saw me as a problem to fix, was someone who understood.' He gives me a keen look. 'You know what I mean?'

I shake my head, although this hits a nerve. Despite our moments, I've never really doubted how lucky I am to have a doctor at home while I am sick. 'Max is extremely brilliant, the second-youngest colorectal consultant surgeon in the country. Very nuanced. In fact, I've never…'

My mouth suddenly dries. I reach out for my water glass. Luigi gets up and limps over towards me.

'Allow me. You need a refill. I trust the tap water downstairs is okay?'

He stands up and I try to hide my shock. The twist to his back and shoulders is very apparent. I do my best not to stare at the dramatic angle of his spine and neck where the spear must have pierced through a gap in his armour.

Of course, I think. How stupid of me. Those portraits of Luigi I had seen would have been painted *before* the battle in Friuli where he'd been injured. I have a flash of that afternoon – six, no, seven years ago? – when I first came across them, diving into the cool darkness of the church off Piazza Brà, in search of some respite from the crushing heat. Hot, itchy and preoccupied, I'd nearly sailed straight past the oil paintings, tucked away in a gloomy side chapel, when the words 'original author of *Romeo and Juliet*' jumped out of the Perspex-framed descriptions.

In the first he was dressed just as he is today, sitting at a desk in front of a piece of parchment, holding a quill and looking thoughtful. In the other he was standing tall in his armour, chest puffed and chin raised under a helmet adorned with a large, proud ostrich feather. In both there was something about his gaze, something that shouldn't have been visible in a flat, Renaissance painting: like he's been waiting forever and can't believe it took me so long to show up.

Walking these days is clearly a painful affair, his left foot landing lightly before he slams down his weight on the right.

'I'm fine,' I say quickly. 'If you just pass me one of those Vitamin C sachets by the clock…'

'If you're worrying about me managing stairs, please don't,' he says sharply. 'My mobility is far better now than it was a few hundred years ago. And not many people can say that.'

I bite my lip. 'No indeed.'

I close my eyes as I listen to Luigi's uneven descent into the kitchen. My apartment, 43a Alvanley Gardens, is a garden flat, a euphemism for what is, in effect, a basement with a glimpse of the sky. The bedroom is raised, the top half of the window looking onto the pavement outside; the kitchen is lower, down a run of nine stairs. So, if you're in the kitchen, you can only see the person in the bedroom above you from the knee-down; from the bedroom you look out at the legs of passers-by on the street.

I can hear cupboards opening and shutting in the kitchen. It's the first chance I've had to really wonder about Luigi being here. Why and *how*. But it's hard to hold on to any thoughts this soon after being in The Pit. My feelings too seem to be turning and reshaping like a kaleidoscope. Gratitude that he's here, and a sharp regret that I'd abandoned him and his story years ago. Fatigue snakes through my system.

I must have dozed, because what seems like a split-second later, he is standing next to my bed with a large wine glass filled with iced water and a sprig of rosemary in one hand. In the other, he holds a plate of sliced salami artfully interleaved with triangles of Pecorino cheese, still with their rinds and drizzled with honey. He presents both with a flourish, like the maître d' of a Michelin-starred restaurant.

'You should come more often.' I push myself up onto one elbow, tucking my hair behind my ear. 'I stopped getting this kind of treatment after the first couple of weeks.'

Luigi's eyes narrow. 'So your doctor friend *doesn't* look after you well? How typical. Ambitious people don't deal well with chronic conditions,' he says, shaking his head knowingly. 'Illness and injury are unbearable for them. All that weakness and waiting.'

'Oh, no, Max is amazing. But he had to get his life back. I encouraged it,' I add quickly. 'He's working hard on setting up a new clinic...'

But Luigi doesn't appear to be listening,

'What you need is to get back in touch with your body again,' he says, gesturing with his hand. 'Do some more living. Get your confidence back. But don't you worry. I'm going to come every day myself. Until my work is done.'

'Your work?'

He gives me a surprised smile. 'Well, of course. Why ever do you think you summoned me after all these years?'

I shake my head.

'To visit, yes,' he says. 'To provide company, moral support, of course. But Vita, *cara*…' he leans a little closer so that I can smell the spicy bite of salami on his breath '… I'm here to release you.'

Release me. Could he really? Free me from this place? A real-life knight in battered armour. Despite my fading senses, I feel a joy so sharp I want to cry out.

His features are beginning to disintegrate. I open my mouth to ask him how, to tell him that I'm ready, that I'll do whatever it takes.

But the poisoned feeling has snagged me by the legs and I lurch backwards into The Pit.

2

A Lark

When I emerge, perhaps minutes, perhaps days later, Max is in bed beside me.

Max's comings and goings to the hospital have always been a movable feast, so they don't mean much to my days, structurally. Except these days if he's here when I wake up, it tends to mean it's the weekend.

'Is it the weekend?'

'Shhh,' he whispers back. 'No. Go back to sleep.'

I open my eyes properly. He's wearing a half-opened, crumpled white shirt and pale blue boxer shorts, his computer resting on his knees. The tendons in his hands flicker as he taps at the keyboard, his face ghostly in the blue light. That force of his concentration, like he is surrounded by some kind of inter-planetary shield, is one of the things I find deeply sexy about him.

'What time is it?'

'You don't want to know,' he murmurs, his eyes still on the screen.

The heavy poisoned feeling has entirely left my system. Sometimes it happens like this: a sudden release as if I've stepped out of a heavy suit of armour. I take a breath, feeling my chest fill easily without the iron breastplate weighing down on it. My fingers, when I wriggle them, are painless and free outside the chainmail gloves. I am giddy with relief. Elated.

'Let's have sex.'

His fingers stop moving instantly. 'Now?' he says, looking over at me. 'You sure that's a good idea?' But he's snapping shut his computer and reaching for me before he's finished the question.

Max is a wonderful kisser. He doesn't kiss like it's the start of something, but like he might find something at the bottom of that kiss that can only be found once. He goes down on me in the same way, like he's searching for treasure. I feel his tongue inside me, feel my insides bloom with heat. At times I wonder if there is something acutely self-conscious in his expertise, like he is aware of how good a lover he is and relishes this so much that he never loses sight of himself in the act. But it's a fleeting thought before my mind empties.

'Is this okay?'

I arch towards him by way of answer. His hands are warm around my hips, his thumbs slot perfectly into the sloping flesh around my pelvic bones. I tell him how good it feels, how he must not stop. When I start to come, I pull him up roughly by the shoulders and push him inside me quickly so that my muscles are still contracting as he starts to move.

'Oh, sweet Jesus,' he says as I tighten myself around him, swallowing him up.

'Did anyone visit today?'

I'm resting my head on Max's chest, which is rising and falling to the bellows of his lungs. He is tracing lazy zig-zags on my forearm with his finger. The blind is open, so you can see the bleed from the city lights. I feel pleasantly tired, not ill tired, though my legs have begun to fizz.

'Huh?' I ask drowsily. 'Are we chatting now?'

Max pokes me. 'Pretend you don't want to pass out straight after sex this time. Just for five minutes. No affection necessary. Just a cold exchange of facts.'

'Define cold.'

'Icy. How was your day?'

I blink up at the ceiling, wondering where to start. What day is it? Or rather, what night? I think of telling him about Luigi... *So, that dead guy I tried to write that screenplay about years ago... he said he'd come to release me*. But it occurs to me how mad this sounds. And besides, I've never gone into detail with Max about the whole Verona episode. It belongs to another time, a closed chapter. My tongue feels thick and heavy at the thought.

'It's okay. Go ahead and sleep,' says Max.

He pushes me gently off his chest and I hear him pad down the stairs to the bathroom where he will wash himself, brush his teeth and floss before coming back to bed. By the time I hear the rush of the taps I feel that I am falling. The colour around me is the blue-grey of thunderstorms and the taste in my mouth is bitter.

When I open my eyes the darkness has lifted a little. I stare at the ceiling for a long while, listening to Max's heavy breathing. He's fallen asleep with the laptop sitting on the bed beside him. I know that he'll have been tinkering with the pitch for the clinic, which he wants to send off to the investors next week. I've read through the slides a few times now and I still don't quite understand what a microbiome is, nor how bespoke testing of people's crap can bring in such eye-watering profits. It's been a little over a year now since Max and I first collided and pretty quickly moved in together. And while the last five, horizontal months have not exactly been a blueprint for romance, I still find his belief in exploring the mysterious universe of the gut rather magical, even if the revolution that it promises in health will come too late to make sense of my particular galaxy of shit.

I catch a movement out of the side of my eye. Looking up, I see Luigi sitting in the chair, one foot jiggling as it rests across his knee.

I nearly fall out of bed. 'Jesus, Luigi,' I say, my heart banging. 'My nervous system is suffering enough as it is.'

'Forgive me, *amore*,' he says, one hand to his heart.

I shake my head. 'I'm glad you're here. I haven't been able to stop thinking about what you said. Please just tell me. How will you do it?'

'Do it?'

'Get me better…' My voice falters a little. 'Release me. That's what you said.'

'Ah!' says Luigi, his face clearing. 'Straight to the marrow, I like that. Well, the first thing you need to know is this: *It is a disease of the blood*.'

I nod quickly. Absolutely, I tell him. I've looked into all of that. Venous blood flow, sticky platelets, clumping, strange markers in blood tests that come and go, and doctors can't seem to explain. I point to my side-table that is heaving with dozens of supplements I've gleaned from YouTube channels and social media posts of functional medics I can't afford: Resveratrol, Ubiquinol, Chlorella, Vitamin C, Vitamin D, Vitamin B3 (flush effect), SAM-e, Creatine, Magnesium, Melatonin, CQ10, fish oil, probiotics, PS-7 mushroom complex, liquid electrolytes. And that was even before the acupuncture, the Chinese herbs and the osteopath who jabbed about my lymph, which he said was like 'a stagnant cistern, let's flush it through!', which brought about the longest time in The Pit I'd had in weeks. 'Of course, everything goes back to inflammation. In fact,' I click my fingers, 'what's the date today? September the sixth, seventh...?'

'You're asking me?'

'I've got this new drug arriving soon from Glasgow that I have real hopes for. It's an off-label thing that's used in bigger doses for drug addicts, but has this amazing side-effect—'

'—but the reality is,' Luigi cuts in, 'medicine hasn't really helped you so far.'

'Not easy to tell,' I say, shaking my head. 'I'm not organised enough, that's the problem. Most days I throw everything at it. Then I can't remember whether I'm feeling better than the day before, and even if I could, I wouldn't know which pills in my pharmacopoeia were actually helping. I'm like Whitney over there,' I say, gesturing at the fishbowl next to him, 'whenever I turn a corner I forget everything that's come before it.'

Luigi glances at Whitney then smiles, leaning his cheek on his fist. A lock of dark hair falls over his eyes. In the dimness of the streetlamps, he looks more arresting than ever, more Roman Emperor than ghost. 'I see so much of myself in you, *cara mia*. Which is why I am the one who can help you.'

'Please, I'm all ears.' I glance over at Max's back. His breathing is deep and even. 'I've been talking too much.'

Luigi clears his throat and starts telling me about the days after the battle, when he was transported, in agony, back to his villa in Montorso where he was taken up to his room, barely conscious, but holding on because Lucina was on her way to visit him.

'You know, of course, that she took one look at the cripple I'd become and broke it off with me?'

I nod quickly. 'I'm sorry.'

'Those first few weeks were the worst kind of hell. They put my legs in metal braces, stuck leeches to my skin until I passed out. One day they carried me outside and strapped me between two trees and tried to stretch me. But all the while, it wasn't the physical pain that hurt the most. I was filled with despair and rage…'

'At Lucina,' I suggest.

'No! At what remained of my broken, twisted body. At myself. For making me repulsive to her; for letting her down. I felt the poison of that shame, the horror of self-hatred. Until the day the lark arrived.'

'A lark? As in… the bird?'

Luigi nods. 'I'd never seen one before. Often heard them, of course. And then one morning, when I was more than usually catatonic, one showed up on my windowsill. Brown-flecked and yellow-bellied, with a darting neck and jet black eyes. It hopped right up to the gap where the window was ajar, in front of my writing desk, and poured a stream of long, trilling notes into the room. It was coaxing me and reprimanding me at the same time. Telling me it had come to wake me. That there was a version of myself that I'd lost in days and weeks of sleep. And the message was clear: *Rise, Luigi. Remember who you are.*'

'And just like that,' I say, my mouth falling open with disbelief, 'you got up and started walking again?'

'Of course not,' he snorts. 'I could barely move a muscle. I still had months of torment ahead before I could walk a single step. But the point was, something in me changed that day. I realised that I needed to stop using all my energy to fight my body and use it instead to fight *for* something.'

'To get her back,' I say slowly.

'Exactly. I was like you, barely thirty. I realised if I could harness that part of me that was young and vigorous, full of love and ideals, I could fight my way out of this. And while I did that, while I forced my body to start working again, I would write a story. And it would be a story with great purpose, the best one I'd ever written.'

My eyes are becoming accustomed to the shadowy light. I feel a familiar twinge of disappointment. Is he, too, saying that it is a matter of will? That if I simply put my mind to it, I could free myself?

'It would be a tale of undying passion,' he continues, his eyes taking on a shining, faraway look, 'based on my and Lucina's own story. I would call it "Giulietta". It would shimmer with such startling beauty and ideals that she would realise what a mistake she had made. She would tell her parents she couldn't go ahead with the marriage they'd arranged for her, and together we'd lead the life we always said we would. Together in my villa in Montorso, where we would raise beautiful children. With her looks and my brains… well, actually, that's not quite fair, *my* looks too—'

He breaks off suddenly as Max flops onto his back with a groan. Then raises his head off the pillow, coughs a few times and rolls back onto his side.

'Don't worry,' I murmur, 'he's still sleeping.' But when I turn back to look at Luigi, the yellow chair is empty.

For what seems like ages, I stay awake, sitting up looking at the chair as if I can will him back. But Luigi doesn't return. Max remains restless. Since he started working on the document for the clinic, his sleep, which has always been bad, has become worse. I'm caught between being proud of his ambition and feeling uneasy about how much more fragmented he seems, always somewhere other than he is, even in sleep.

Ambitious people don't deal well with chronic conditions… I'd never had an ambitious boyfriend before Max. What was it that Luigi called Danny Cousins? *That wonderful artist who makes worlds.* I have a flash of us sitting together under heavy beams in a dark-panelled restaurant in Verona, him in that awful corduroy jacket and his five-day-old beard, laughing at my expression as the couple at the table next to us were brought two horse steaks in a dark gravy and slabs of polenta coated in lard. I'd been fretting about what to do with my career when Danny's expression turned solemn. He'd reached for my hand across the table and told me that the point was not what job you choose in life, but *where it takes you*. Whether it allows you to stay free and tasting the pleasures of life, not in a rut. And how he was sorry now that he'd chosen the job in Verona over the one he'd been offered in Rome, because in Rome they are less into eating lard and horses and more into offal, and he'd pay a lot to see my face in front of a bowl of pasta swimming with guts that have little suckers all over them.

Then I think of Luigi's lark. *Rise, remember who you are.*

I feel my eyes spring open. Was that why Luigi had shown up after all these years: to remind me of a version of myself I had lost? And was Danny Cousins the key to this somehow: Danny, who Luigi had mentioned so casually, but was now knocking about in my mind, like the answer to a question I couldn't quite fully grasp?

I look for my phone and realise it is plugged into the charger on Max's side of the bed. Being careful not to touch him, I stretch over and take it off the cable. A blue light fills the room. Max shifts a little and then settles again. I breathe out, open my email app and click Compose.

Dear Danny,

Weird getting an email from me, I know.

I pause, thinking.

Do you still have photos of that villa we visited just outside Verona? You remember how I was obsessed with Luigi da Porto, the guy who wrote the story of Romeo and Juliet before Shakespeare? It started off as an alibi to hang out with you in Verona while you had an actual job. I thought I could impress the hell out of you by writing some kooky but brilliant film script that would take Cannes Film Festival by storm…

Too try-hard. I hold down the delete button until all but the first line disappears. Then glance over at Whitney Houston who is staring at me, tail wafting slowly, suspended in the broken arch.

You've often come to mind over the years. But more so lately. For some reason Luigi has—

My thumb hovers again. I delete the last two words, replace them.

—our time in Verona has come back to haunt me. Anyway, it would be great to catch up. Shall we make a plan to chat on the phone?

I sign off with a single initial (familiar, even a little suggestive, though you couldn't pin anything on me) and am rereading for the second time when Max rolls over again.

'Are you okay?' he murmurs.

My thumb freezes mid-scrolling.

'Fine.'

'You sure?' His hand reaches out to squeeze mine. 'You're not in those forums again? They'll make you mad at this time of night.'

'No,' I say. 'I promise.'

Max wouldn't mind me emailing an ex. He's not easily threatened, something I find both annoying and attractive. 'You think you'd like me to be more jealous,' he once told me. 'But you'd be flattered for a moment and then find me weak and claustrophobic.' At the time I'd grunted in disagreement, but we both knew he was right.

I wait until his breathing deepens again, then press Send.

That night, I sleep badly. Whenever I wake up, I look at the yellow armchair where Luigi was sitting. Yesterday, was it? Today? My head aches, as if some kind of foreign object has lodged itself in my psyche.

The fact that I haven't told Max about Luigi's visit feels strange. A departure of some kind. I look at his back, at the wings of his shoulder blades and the curve of his strong forearm resting on the sheet. Those arms that climb mountains and save lives.

'Do you like climbing?' Max asked me, soon after we met.

And I said, 'Are you kidding? I *love* climbing.' Which, given the fact that we were in such early stages of courtship, could easily have been a lie. But, as it happened, was true.

What I didn't tell Max – because I find it hard to speak casually about my upbringing and so tend to duck referencing it – was that when Gracie and I were kids, climbing was the closest we ever got to feeling safe. The giant flowering chestnut tree that grew out of our neighbour's garden was our territory, away from our stepmother Faye and her son Magnus. Faye with her whitewashed world and obsession with order. Those precisely stacked cushions. And Magnus with his broad, blond freckled face and piercing blue eyes, one with a squint, who ignored us completely except if we were already watching TV and he wanted a different channel. In which case he'd snatch the remote and say, 'Scoot, rugrats!' Swinging through that chestnut was the only time Gracie and I felt out of reach of them both; safer, on higher ground.

Which is a roundabout way of saying that when Max suggested a climbing weekend in Wales a few weeks into dating, I thought I had it in the bag. I envisioned something like the last scene of *The Sound of Music*, us walking through rugged hills, a proper hike with bits of clambering, but not so out of breath that we couldn't chat. It wasn't until we arrived and he unloaded all of his kit under what he'd billed as a 'small practice run' that I realised how completely out of my depth I was. I stared up at the sheer incline, then down at the pile of crampons and pitons and wedges and tapers (none of which I knew by name at the time) with dismay.

Max was a good teacher, making it fun even though it had begun to rain. But after about an hour of frustration – in which I had just started to make some progress on the basics but then turned my ankle painfully and was determined not to show it – I lost heart and sat down. At which point Max, clearly itching to use his real skills, suggested he give me a bit of a demo.

At first, it was fun to watch. Sexy. The speed with which he made little calculations, the deftness with which he moved from one foothold to the next, his back muscles moving like liquid beneath his t-shirt, the grace with which he seemed to float up the rockface like he was solving a vertical puzzle.

And then, just as suddenly, I started to resent him. Something about the pain in my ankle and my wounded pride rubbed up against such a supreme display of self-sufficiency and began to flicker into a kind of rage. Standing below with a crick in my neck as he moved inexorably upwards, and the rain pounded down, plastering my hair around my face, I was aware not just that I wasn't needed, but that I no longer existed for him. And I thought: *If this is what it's like, being with someone who is so utterly sure of themself that they never have to pause or look down or ask for help, then it's not for me.*

Later, in a pub, drinking lager shandies and eating roasted peanuts with my ankle throbbing quietly below the table, it all felt a bit less dramatic. And so I told him: 'That sense of certainty you must have, to be a surgeon and to scale a mountain, I kind of hate you for it. Which I know is my failing, and makes me a lesser mortal, but I feel I should tell you as I guess this means we may not be such a good fit.' As I said it, I felt a momentary pain around my heart, as if someone was squeezing it, and then a sudden relief.

He tipped back his head and laughed.

'Can't see the joke?' I said. And then, when he didn't stop, 'Max, I mean it. What's so funny?'

He shook his head, smiling. 'How can you be so clever and so wrong at the same time?'

I munched on more peanuts. 'I don't see how I'm wrong or clever,' I muttered. 'Not in this instance, anyway.'

He laughed again and took my hand. His knuckles had some raw grazes across them; when he squeezed his hand, the skin under them went white. I had to resist snatching my own away.

'If you would allow yourself to get to know me, you'd see it's just the opposite,' he said gently. 'I'm full of doubt. Riddled with it. I wrestle it every time I walk into a hospital, let alone pick up a scalpel. Climbing is about the only time it goes away.'

I glanced at him then, but he was looking at me with such a rooted, steady gaze that I immediately looked away again.

'Vita?'

I nodded, not trusting my voice.

It had never happened this way before. Me, with another person. Normally I was breathing life into something that I knew didn't quite exist. This time I was fighting every step, but still, it pulled me forward.

3

Never a Cross Word

Max hasn't moved in the bed at all, which is unusual for him. I wonder if he gave up earlier and took a sleeping pill, pinning himself to oblivion.

I look back at the ceiling, watching it light up from the headlamps of the occasional passing car. Bright, brighter, then dark again. Each time one passes, I allow myself to pick up my phone and refresh my inbox. As if, somewhere else in the world, a star-crossed Danny Cousins is also checking his email in the middle of the night. The rest of the time, I let my mind travel. Taking me back, as it so often does, to that day in Brighton, not long before the world went dark.

A studio flat, not far from Brighton pier, in early April. It's the third of April in fact. Two weeks before I move in with Max, less than a month before I fall sick. At this stage, I still don't believe in ghosts.

'You're getting too skinny again,' I tell my sister, perching on one of the packing boxes and swinging my legs so that the heels of my trainers bump against the cardboard. We've driven one load of stuff up to her new place in London and the flat is nearly empty. Just the bed, the fridge, some taped-up boxes. It's a process I've been through many times over the years with Gracie and each time her 'new start' has felt a little less believable, like a second-hand car salesman shooting his cuffs and talking that little bit too loud.

But this feels different, somehow.

I've taken twenty-four hours off work to come and help her finish packing up. Once we're done with the heavy lifting, there are a couple of things to do before I take the 20.17 back to Waterloo. Chiefly, dye her roots ('My natural colour,' says Gracie, holding up the Pink Pixie box) and take a farewell stroll down her favourite stretch of beach.

Gracie still doesn't look up from the back page of the newspaper, which is folded quarter-size. She is lying on her belly on the bare floorboards chewing the end of a Biro, spinning it between her teeth and biting down hard enough so you can hear the plastic cracking.

'*Possessing one* could mean "I" in the middle of the word,' she mutters. 'What's another word for "spirit"?'

No matter what state she is in, we've never stopped doing the crossword together. Gracie would say that we search for clever words that mean nothing in place of all the things that go unspoken. I think we both just like a problem we can solve.

'Ghost,' I suggest automatically. 'Spook.' I wince as her pen cracks again. 'You see, gnawing on that Biro. Obviously craving starchy carbs.'

My younger sister has always been too thin. Food has never much interested her. Mealtimes are just another event littered with risks for the epileptic: knives and corners of tables; scalding liquids; food to choke on. Sometimes the sight of her body fills me with guilt and sorrow, its fragility a reminder of everything I didn't do to protect her. Other times I suspect she enjoys it, this power of vanishing in plain sight.

'Unlikely,' says Gracie, rubbing the end of her nose like she's trying to scrub dirt off it. 'Whole word has got to be "frenzy". What's another word for "food shop"? Grocery, bakery, butchers… something shorter… stall?'

There's a rim of black ink around her lips from the Biro. Somehow it doesn't make her look as shit as it would other people. She writes the letters higgledy-piggledy on a space next to the crossword and cocks her head.

'I thought *I* was supposed to be the one in the family who dodges questions,' I say.

Still no eye contact.

'Gracie!'

'Not a question,' she says eventually.

I frown, bumping my heels more loudly. 'Come again?'

'You said, "You're getting too skinny again." No upward inflection to your voice. Ergo, an assertion, not a question.'

My little sister uses words like 'ergo' and 'parentheses' that no one in this century uses. When we were teens, I suspected she was a genius. Later I found it embarrassing. It took me a while to twig that she wasn't just being pretentious. Even though she was faster on the draw in an argument than any of us, it came from academic insecurity. She was kicked out of two schools and one sixth-form college for drugs and truancy; the Latin and the long words started the summer I aced my GCSEs.

'*And* again,' I say, triumphantly. 'Titanic dodge of subject.'

Gracie looks up with a sigh. It's funny. I know you're supposed to grow out of thinking your sister is the most beautiful girl in the world, but I've never been able to shake it off. Even at her lowest ebb she never loses her poise, a certain grace with which she holds her long neck, the quick laughter in her eyes that makes you want to be with her more than with other people. Even when she's irritating the hell out of you.

'Got out of the wrong side of bed this morning,' she suggests, flashing me a look.

'Lazy use of a commonly used phrase. Ergo, cliché.'

But it's true. I do feel anxious, borderline irritable. At first, I thought it was because I couldn't quite afford the time off work, that I knew it would be a scramble on the train ride home to bash out a brief for the new episode of *Confessions* (our subject this week, a Tour de France champion and much-fancied *enfant terrible* who took months to land). But it's dawning on me, as the day goes by, that what's bothering me most is my growing optimism.

This time Gracie really does seem to be at a turning point. The promise of a new job and a flat share with a grounded friend, both of which I can see lasting, a move that is more about running towards life than away from it. But I've been around for the turning of enough of Gracie's 'new leaves' to know better, so along with my burgeoning hope comes a fretful resentment.

I lean over and pick up some brown envelopes from a scattered pile on the floor.

'Tell me these are not all from the same fine?' I say, hearing the haughty older-sister tone invade my voice. 'You know you only need to pay half if you pay within four weeks?'

'Which is nothing compared to the insurance premium I'm shelling out for these days,' she flashes back.

I bite my lip. 'Ouch! I know I owe you for that.'

Gracie laughs. 'I love it when I make you blush. Actually, I've decided when I get to London I'll swap in my car for a more charming banged-up one. You remember how Dad used to say wardens would never give Mr Banks a ticket because they felt too bad about it?'

'Who's Mr Banks?'

Gracie gives me an odd look. 'You can't be serious?'

I shake my head slowly. '*Mary Poppins*?'

'Jesus Christ, Vita.' She puts the paper and her pen down. 'The Deux Chevaux… the umbrella car. Green-and-white, the folding roof with the poppers, the one that Dad kept until… *You know.*'

'Oh, sure. Mr Banks,' I say, with a light laugh and then look away because she'll know that I'm bullshitting. That I did forget all about Mum's old car, let alone its name, and that thinking about it now – flashes from an era before Faye came onto the scene – makes me want to stick both my fingers in my ears and start humming loudly.

I stretch over to pick up the newspaper. 'Where are we… five across? *Frenzy in food shop, spirit possessing one.* Surely "frenzy" means anagram. How many letters is it… eight… so it could be…'

'I think you're making a big mistake,' says Gracie.

'Well, hold your horses. How many letters does "possessing" have? One, two, three…'

'Vita!'

I look up.

'You're making a mistake moving in with Max. He's not right for you.'

The moment jars. I blink, startled that she's gone there. My sister and I don't talk about Max these days. We tease and bait each other, both bloody-minded, both competing for the last word. Both aware of the treacherous undercurrents without naming them. But she's stopped talking about my relationship and in turn I don't say, 'What the hell are you doing with your life? When are you going to stop pretending to yourself that you're the "liberated" one?'

This then is a breach of contract. I feel something in the room shift.

'Are you going to take that back?'

It's not escaped my attention that my sister's attitude to Max has changed. (He's remarked on it too, a couple of times, in an 'Am-I-being-paranoid way?') But I've struggled to understand it. To begin with, they bonded so fast, I was almost jealous. If Max is clear-eyed about me, Gracie is clairvoyant and they would delight in the common ground they stomped around on, teasing me. But the last couple of times we've all hung out together, it's been different. Like she's forgotten a shared language they'd been learning together. At best, missing his cues.

Once or twice, I've wondered whether I should bring it up, but always baulked at potential outcomes. That's the problem with Gracie. Stressful emotions can leave her open to one of the epileptic fits always lurking in the shadows nearby, an intruder with a baseball bat, poised to attack.

'No,' says Gracie. 'Won't take it back. On the contrary. I think as soon as you move in, he'll ask you to marry him. And even though you've only been together for five minutes…'

'Nine months.'

'… you'll get hitched for all the wrong reasons and end up…'

'End up?' I echo dangerously.

She holds my gaze. 'End up in the wrong story like me.'

A fist of rage forms in my chest. I throw the paper onto the ground where it lands with a slap. 'I'm not like you,' I say, my jaw aching from keeping my voice low.

Gracie rolls over and sits up. Her face is strangely lit up. 'No, Vita. You're not like me. By all appearances your life is pretty tidy. But until you work out how to stop shape-shifting for your boyfriend, let alone dressing up other people's lives for that fucked-up podcast…' Here she sucks in another breath, two spots of colour appearing on her high cheekbones. 'Until you stop hiding from our past, and turn round and face it, on some level we're the same, you and me.'

Here they are, the words she carries around in her pockets like hand grenades. I want to open my mouth and start shouting but the stakes are too high, so instead I bang my heels hard against the packing boxes, my ears burning.

'And Max,' I say, with low fury. 'What makes him a part of this?'

I don't look up as she answers, so I can't see her face. 'If you can't tell that, you've really forgotten who you are.'

Another tense silence.

'Not sure you're right about the anagram,' says Gracie in a different voice. Looking up, I see she's walking towards me, having picked up the newspaper. The other hand reaching out for mine, an olive branch.

I look my little sister in the eye.

'Fuck you,' I say, snatching my hand away.

Then I stand up and walk out.

I'm halfway to the train station when it comes to me. *Delirium.* 'I' in 'rum'. Shop as in *deli.*

Delirium. I have a flash of Gracie foaming and jerking on the floor.

Shit! I think. *Shit.*

Always the guilt.

I turn around and walk slowly back. I still have keys to her flat and let myself in.

She hasn't moved.

'Delirium,' I say.

It only takes her a moment. 'Frenzy in food shop,' she says. 'Clever.' She looks at me as if to apologise but doesn't.

'I don't want to talk about it,' I say. 'Not a fucking word unless you take it all back.'

She nods, pale-faced, and we hug a little stiffly.

I sit down on the bare floorboards, back to the wall, and she follows suit. For a moment or two we sit in silence, side by side. Then she reaches for my left arm, rolls up my sleeve and tells me to close my eyes.

It's a game we always played as kids. She tickles her fingers very slowly up my arm. I have to say 'when' as she reaches the mole in the crook of my elbow. As always, I call it much too early.

'Way off.' She grins as I open my eyes.

I can't help it, I laugh too. Her hand is still resting on my arm, and I take it.

It's a sticking plaster rather than a resolution. I know it won't hold for long.

That's the problem about us: all the things that bind us so tight one moment, can strangle us the next. The last time she and I argued, we didn't speak again for months.

4

The Wrong Medicine

'Is that excrement?' says Luigi, leaning forward in the yellow armchair and staring into Whitney's bowl with great interest.

I glance over. There's a long brown string that Whitney's dragging from her midriff, and I mean really long. This happens a fair bit. The first time I noticed it, I thought it must be something else – because who swims around dragging a piece of shit twice the length of their body? Unless we're talking psychologically, in which case, ask Gracie.

'Yes, it's shit,' I sigh. 'I've looked it up. When it becomes long and string-like it's because they're constipated from overeating.'

'Ah,' says Luigi, nodding. 'So you're a feeder.'

'No, I'm not,' I snap, because this touches a nerve. It's something Gracie says about me. 'It's just hard to keep track of goldfish meals when time has melted and most of the day you're lying in the bottom of a well… I'm sorry.' I exhale. 'Of course, you understand this better than I do.'

'No better than you,' he says, smiling. 'But, Vita, I do understand you. We've known each other a long time after all.'

And as he says this, the strangest thing happens. With that smile I find myself back in the cool darkness in Verona, the sound of my footsteps echoing on the stone floor of the church, the smell of candle wax and my eyes still adjusting from the dazzling light outside. But as I walk into the side chapel, instead of the paintings of Luigi I expect to find there, I see a series of living photographs, framed moments from my life. Moments when I have felt, just for an instant, that I was sharing the exact same experience in the universe with another person: my sister and I lying in the attic in a cold holiday house talking about our stepmother; my mother smiling at me the first time I tied my own shoelaces; holding hands with two college friends at a funeral; exchanging life stories on a train in Mexico with a woman I met while travelling; for a heartbeat, I see them all there as I feel that absolute connection of gut and soul in Luigi's smile. Then I blink, and he's gone.

The clock says 5.47. The yellow chair is empty again and I can see Max's jumper flung over one of its arms. This time, I feel a real sense of loss. The room is gloomy in that way that happens just before sunrise, but also sunset, so it takes me a while to realise that it's actually early evening and I must have slept the whole night and then the day afterwards too. My focus keeps shifting in and out, and I realise that this moment is just a brief release to the surface. I'm still in The Pit.

I'm back down here.

A feeling of extreme weakness like I might dis a p p e a r.

Every cell is squeezed dry leaving just a

frail web of nerves

the skeleton of a leaf.

An itch on my nose. No energy to lift my hand.

Hard to distinguish weakness from lack of signals from the brain

On the other side of a wall transparent but impenetrable like thick glass I can see all the things I should be doing

(Breathe)

(Stretch)

(Message a friend)

(Put music on)

But can no more reach any of these than push my fist through the glass wall

Phone ringing now...

This is the time of day that Gracie would always ring. Perhaps I should pick up, the silence between us has gone on far too long. Longer than any of the 'breaks' we've had before. I picture her name flashing on the phone screen. *Gracie (new phone).* So long now since that day in Brighton when we argued about Max. Not a word since. I imagine her, sitting in the new flat just above the cheap accessories shop, balancing her phone between ear and shoulder as she wanders around in her t-shirt and knickers, waiting for me to pick up. I want to reach for the phone, to hear her voice, but I can't, I know I can't. Or maybe I could, of course I could, all I need to do is reach out my hand.

She's the very last person I can talk to. Or maybe that's not true. Perhaps of all people, Gracie would understand what's happening to me best, would know that it's not just lingering symptoms, it's not just a bit of tiredness; it's a poison and panic and pain in your system, a waxing and waning of self, a bleakness rising from the abyss. Call it what you like: post-viral-syndrome-chronic-fatigue-lyme-disease-long-covid-myalgic-encephalomyelitis-fibromyalgia. Gracie, please tell me, amIgoingmadamIgoingmadamIgoingmadamI

going…

going…

gone

The phone rings off abruptly.

The quietness brings relief.

Sometime later, the buzzer goes next to my head. My mouth tastes bitter, like I've been sucking on copper coins. I stare out of the half-window onto the street and see a pair of eighties black leather biker boots and a few inches of chunky leather-clad calf on the top doorstep. A quick body scan tells me I've popped back up from The Pit unscathed this time, without that odd, poisoned weakness, or the aches in my legs that can last for hours. I fumble for the buzzer Max had installed a few weeks after I got sick, but before I stopped the visitors.

'Medication,' says a voice.

I swing my feet to the floor immediately.

The only delivery I'm expecting is the medicine that I told Luigi about. I discovered it on one of the many nights I spent trawling online forums for panaceas. The chemist said it takes up to two weeks for delivery: it must be ten days already. *Try not to get too excited.*

But I have that manic surge of elation and optimism that sometimes follows a good exit from The Pit. My hands are shaking a little as I pull Max's jacket over my pyjamas. Out of all the increasingly elaborate interventions I've researched recently – the oxygen therapies; the plasma transfusions; an electric horse massager that you strap on your arm – this one seems the least crazy and most affordable.

The stairs up to the ground floor look unfamiliar. In the last few months, I've been outside my flat a total of six times, always for doctors (not counting the times Max plonked me in a patch of sunshine in the garden, a blanket over my legs). I had barely moved in before I fell sick, and before that whenever I visited him I never lingered long enough to really register the carpet, which is one of those dingy, disappearing oatmeal colours and curls up at the edges, or the scratched skirting that's collected a little heap of dust along its ledge. According to one of the GPs, I'm supposed to climb stairs slowly, even when I *don't* have symptoms. Stop for frequent rests when I should count one mississippi two mississippi three mississippi up to twenty times in my head. But I keep picturing the courier giving up and driving off with my miracle cure to some depot with miles of stacked shelving that I won't be able to locate for weeks. So I move as fast as I can up the stairs, down the hallway, up to the heavy front door.

The courier is still there, holding a padded envelope. Although he hasn't flipped up his mirrored visor, I beam at him. It's the first time I've been out of the flat by myself for months, let alone stood on the threshold to the outside world, and I feel filled with sudden hope. I want to tell him that the weak evening sun straining through the low grey clouds is beautiful, and the fact that he can make his body do anything he wants, like ride a motorbike or walk to the shops without pain, is a miracle also. He just doesn't know it because life tricks you that way. You only know how much you owe to your health when you see it disappearing in the rear-view mirror. But if you could… if you could only look down and see it now…

'Right here, lady. Don't have all day.' I pick up the little stick-pen to sign on the screen. That's when I see the delivery is addressed to Mrs. S. Rothwell, the piano teacher upstairs. My stomach lurches with disappointment.

'It's for my neighbour.'

The leather jacket creaks with impatience. 'But you'll sign for her?'

The stick-pen hovers for a moment. In the last few weeks, I've not wanted to see anyone, let alone strangers. The idea of ringing the doorbell of a neighbour I haven't yet met makes me feel a bit queasy. On the other hand, I'll walk right past the door to her maisonette on the way back downstairs. It seems churlish not to take it.

I'm a few steps away from Mrs Rothwell's front door when I hear the piano.

Our shared house (she has the top two floors) is a Victorian mid-terrace with thin walls and draughty doors, so I'm not surprised by how clearly I can hear it, like it's sitting right out in the hallway.

It's a piece of music I've heard coming through the ceiling several times – perhaps the one that Luigi was describing. What was it he said… a *flow of arpeggios… that haunting melody buried in between…* yes, this must be it. I remember the curve of his hand through the air as if he was conducting while he described it. Though who the composer was, I can't recall. *Liszt*, that was it. Something about a dream.

I pause in the corridor, transfixed, the parcel forgotten in my hand.

Since I've been ill, it feels like my hearing has sharpened. I've got better at tuning into all the noises around me. The footsteps of people passing on the pavement, which I try to decipher before they come into view: the ticking of heels or the flat slap of loafers, the squeak of children's trainers or the clicking claws of a trotting dog. Car doors opening or slamming; the thunder of bin day. And the sounds coming from within the building that you have to guess at fast, before they bewilder or begin to torment you. The ticking of radiators and the high keening of a pipe, the moan of a floorboard or the wind rattling old window frames. And strangest of all, a humming vibration when I lie awake at night, which I fancy is the voice of the walls themselves, holding their space within the clamour of the city.

Above all, though, it's the piano that's been the soundtrack to my illness. Whether it's the stumbling notes of children plonking out the same musical phrases (try *that* with a post-viral migraine) or the rarer, virtuoso flights of the teacher.

Listening to her play now, without the muffling of the floor between us, is a completely different affair.

The melody is slowing now, the left hand walking down the keyboard in single, exquisitely mournful notes. Slow, slower still, and then building up again, quicker, now urgent, and then shifting into a ripple of high chords, like a wave breaking, that leave us on higher, more hopeful ground.

Having never met Mrs Rothwell, all I know about her are the bare facts, passed on by Max who has lived downstairs from her for over a year. That she is relatively old but still sprightly, has recently lost her husband. (Perhaps that's the 'heartbreak' Luigi was referencing in her music?) I think of an old lady sitting at the piano, bony fingers flying over the keys, transporting herself to a time when her husband was alive, perhaps when they were much younger together. Moments together she can evoke, but never get back.

It's only when the piece finishes that I wake up to where I am. Standing in the corridor in my makeshift pyjamas and slippers, tears streaming down my face. Revisited by a feeling that I cannot, dare not, name.

'Dear girl,' says Luigi, as soon as I open the door to the basement flat. 'Do sit down.'

He's at my kitchen table, legs propped up on another chair and cape swept back from one shoulder, eating from a paper bag of purplish-black grapes.

'Muscadines, not grapes,' he says, waving the bag. 'More like berries, scientifically speaking. They're native to the New World, though we cultivate plenty ourselves these days. Most importantly, they're full of remarkable healing properties and they taste like first love.' He pops a couple in his mouth, closes his eyes. 'At least, the flesh does. You suck that out, then get rid of the seeds and skins like so. A good workout for the tongue, which sadly is not as useful for me as it once was.' He spits delicately into a cupped hand. At the sound of the piano upstairs, he looks up. 'I was right, was I not, about the virtuoso? The feeling she is putting into that piece. Of someone who has left their heart somewhere else entirely… Tell me, *cara*, what is that rather enticing parcel you have there?'

I glance down at Mrs R's medication.

By now, my legs feel like they have moved to a different side of the room than the rest of me. There is no pain this time, but rather a complete absence of strength, like a scarecrow that's had all its stuffing yanked out. I drop down into one of the chairs opposite Luigi and sling the Jiffy bag on the table.

'Not for me, sadly,' I say. 'I'm going to take it back upstairs.'

Luigi plants both feet on the ground and leans forward to peer at the address.

'You just *were* upstairs.'

'It didn't feel like the right moment to lean on the bell.'

'Quite right,' he agrees, rustling around for another muscadine. 'Interesting, though, with all those "Private" stickers on it. I wonder what it is.'

'Just medicine. I was hopeful it was the stuff from Scotland I was telling you about.'

'So, she is sick,' says Luigi thoughtfully.

'Or just old. Old folk take quite a lot of painkillers.'

Luigi has picked up the parcel and is examining it.

'Don't you find those stickers *actively* make you want to snoop? Especially rule-breakers like you and me. Also, why does it need to be "Private *and* Confidential"? Hammering the point home rather, isn't it?'

I open my mouth to agree when suddenly I've drifted off to somewhere else entirely. Standing in Gracie's bedroom in our old house holding her diary, which has PRIVATE! and KEEP OUT! in bubble writing all over the cover. My heart is thumping and I'm listening out for footsteps because I've always sworn blind that I'd never read it. But she hasn't spoken to me in two days and I'm desperate to see what she's thinking.

I flick through the last few pages. I know the words I'm looking for, apart from my own name, that is. Words like 'coward' and 'weak' and 'traitor'. But she hasn't written about me. Somehow, this is worse. There's no mention of me at all, apart from the bare fact that I'd sneaked on her to Faye, our stepmother. The rest is all about her. How she's never quite sure what she's afraid of, but that's all she can really think about when she knows Faye's in the house: a nameless dread that she's done something wrong, that Faye will come and find her and make her feel worthless. About the fact she's sure that Faye hates her the most, that she can see it in her eyes; that Faye wants to break her, perhaps because she's the youngest, perhaps because she thinks she can make Gracie her creature. And how the day I'd snitched on her, Faye went hunting around the house to track her down. How Gracie had hidden in the wardrobe in the spare room, but she was shaking so much she had to grip onto the hangers to stop them from jangling and giving her away.

I look up. Luigi is smiling at me tenderly. I feel a rush of self-consciousness.

'Do you really think of me as a rule-breaker? I mean, did you? Back then?'

He laughs. 'Of course! You and Danny were always up to no good. Breaking into that castello at night and sitting up on that terrifying high wall, smoking whatever it was. Jumping into the moat and scaring the hell out of that poor night watchman. And remember that fancy fish restaurant in Lago di Garda where you did a runner? I do mean rule-breaking in the best possible way, my dear. People who are happy to cross lines and bend a few rules here and there. Who are spirited and curious.'

My gaze follows his to the sticker on the Jiffy bag. *Private and Confidential.* By the time I look up, there's no trace of Luigi or his muscadines at the table, only an empty chair, pushed out at an angle.

I push the parcel over to the far side of the table.

The weak, trembly feeling again. What if I never get my stuffing back? What if I'm stuck like this for years, a spineless sack of dust who talks to pompous ghosts; an old invalid in the prime of my life, reduced to rubble after a short walk to the front door? What if I can never go for a brisk walk again, never swim, never drive, never get to have a family? Never. Never. Never.

Stop.

Breathe.

Remember Whitney Houston.

5

The Flood

It's raining down here
Warm
s l o w
f a t
drops
the kind before a storm breaks.
Some [   ] in my memory because I'm no longer
wait, that's not true
Still sick, bedbound, but somewhere else
I can feel the rain, hear the crickets humming
A treehouse in the jungle. Struck down by a tropical illness, which also makes every bone in my body ache
Malaria?   Dengue fever?
Need to think straight
On a mission to find botanical cure for the mystery illness that is confounding the the the
My bedroom has no [   ]

Come on, *come on*
It has no
            OO
       R   F

which is why
        I can feel
                the   pat-ter
        of   rain-drops
        Funny, though
        no stars
        And surely even a monsoon wouldn't

I fumble for the bedside table, switch on the light. *The Pit. Whitney Houston.* Breathe slowly. Don't panic. A deep crash, that's all. Brain reconfiguring. Objects becoming words. Goldfish. Mezzanine. Max's flat. Rain.

I look up.

Across the ceiling, directly above my head, long, rusty streaks of damp follow the grid shape of pipes. And there's water dripping through. Really quite a lot of water.

Not long before my mother died, before her headaches were even mentioned, we went on a sailing holiday. I don't remember much about the trip except that one morning when we woke up the sky was slate-grey and the sea was very angry. Our boat suddenly felt flimsy and lurched from side to side, sending up banks of spray and taking our stomachs with it. Gracie was very small and slept through most of it, but I sat in the swaying hull with my mother who was teaching me how to tie knots. (Looking back, I see she must have been trying to distract me.) I remember her saying, 'You can't tell if someone is a good sailor until you see them in a storm.'

Mrs Rothwell's bathroom is directly above our bedroom. I know this because I can hear water thundering through the pipes most mornings at around 11 a.m. when she runs a bath. And then the clanking about an hour later when the water sluices out.

Warm water drips down onto my bed, gathering pace. 6.10. It must be early evening. No sign of Luigi.

I think: a good sailor would get dressed quickly, but without haste, put a bucket under the leak and go upstairs to knock on their neighbour's door. But none of this happens.

My brain does not click into action.

I'm not hyper-alert, yet possessed with a sudden, decisive calm.

I am not a good sailor.

Instead, I watch the stain inch across the ceiling, following its progress like I'm betting on a snail race, and observing the not unpleasant drowsiness that sometimes spreads through me post-Pit. Possibly I doze, because within moments, it seems, the clock shows 6.23, then 6.36.

These are the times when I feel most like an imposter. Not recovered, but not ill either. Outside of myself, somehow. Languishing.

A wave of self-disgust rolls through me, and I ride it all the way back to the first hospital visit, five weeks after this started. Sitting on a hard chair in a corridor that smells of bleach, just outside the room where a doctor, a colleague of Max's, is consulting with him about my latest set of blood results. I hear the scrape of a chair leg as they confer around his computer. Murmured conversation.

'Everything's bang in range,' he is saying. 'There's nothing wrong with her.'

And Max is agreeing: 'Yes… yes, I can see that.'

Then the other doctor again, asking if I've tried antidepressants.

'Not yet,' Max tells him. 'Though she has a history.'

Eventually I reach for my phone, find Max on WhatsApp. *Water coming through the ceiling. Lots.*

Then I go back to watching the stain creep across the paintwork. The straight lines of damp that follow the pipes have started to billow on either side. It looks like some kind of fungi, blooming with magical speed.

I have a sudden vision of the ceiling cracking: jagged hairlines spreading outwards like a giant egg hatching, before the entire bath, complete with a naked Mrs

Rothwell in a shower cap and a huge gush of soapy water, comes crashing down on top of me.

It's 6.48 p.m. Nothing back from Max. I can see by the two little grey ticks that the message has landed, but I don't know whether he has read it or not, as he disabled that function after an incident with a stalker patient.

Once when we were in bed, listening to the sound of water rushing through Mrs Rothwell's pipes, we had an argument about the kind of people who like very long baths. Max's view was that lolling about in baths is an exercise in self-indulgence. My view was that people who hurry out of showers have inner lives that frighten them. It came to a head with me shouting that I could never love someone who couldn't spend a happy hour in a bath. That anyone who rushed in and out of the shower, even when they weren't in a rush, was spiritually bankrupt.

I'm not sure whose idea it was to have make-up sex in the bath. But after that he came round to my point of view (the more time spent in them, the better).

Now I find a *Singing in the Rain* gif with Gene Kelly in a downpour, endlessly twirling round a lamp-post, and send it to Max with a message: *Hurry home, bring umbrella.*

Sending this seems like an accomplishment.

I lie back and watch the fungus spread.

*

Still no reply from Max. I call him to see if it rings, which it does for a while before clicking through to voicemail, which means he's not in surgery yet. So either not checking or ignoring. I think for a moment and type, *Is that a damp patch on your side of the bed or are you just pleased to see me?* Max is strangely prudish about rude jokes, which, for someone who spends half his day delving around in people's arseholes – I tell him – is oddly charming.

The water is dripping through in several places now. Almost all of it is landing on Max's side of the bed, funnily enough. Who else to ring? None of my friends is remotely practical. My family: forget it. Gracie would see the funny side of it, but not these days. Danny Cousins was great in a crisis, but considering he hasn't yet hit Reply to my email, the chances of him riding to the rescue feel slim to pathetic.

The fact that Danny seems to be ghosting me bothers me more than I thought it would. Even when I'm not thinking about him, I have a sense of permanent peripheral irritation, like a sneeze that won't come. Even internet stalking is proving difficult. Further Googling has revealed that there are several more Danny Cousinses out there, though no operatic set designers either going by Danny or Daniel. Instead, I've found a financial adviser in Dubai, a web-marketing consultant in Canada, a retiree in Barcelona, a psychoanalytic therapist in Minnesota, a receptionist in Edmonton, a firefighter in California, a boat builder in New Zealand and an inflatables manufacturer in Scotland. (Out of all of them, I'd prefer him to be the boat builder, though maybe the therapist would be able to tell me why the whole thing has been bothering me so much.)

Of course, it's possible he's using a different email address now. Though why wouldn't it have bounced back? Or perhaps he is finally working in a staff position somewhere and rarely checks his personal mail. (This feels more unlikely – Danny always swore that he would remain freelance and never become a salary man, because what's the point of doing something creative if you're not your own boss?) Most likely then, it's deliberate.

Which leaves who to call on? Luigi? My actual knight-in-shining armour, who come to think of it, told me he'd be visiting every day. What point is a confidant if he doesn't show up when you need him?

'You could use Whitney's bowl,' comes a muffled voice. 'To catch the drips.'

I look over at the yellow armchair where Luigi is lounging, using a toothpick to dig something out of his molars. Whatever it is, it's very stubbornly lodged. Probably the muscadine pits.

'Where have you been?' I ask, with an edge of irritation.

'Sorry,' he says, examining the toothpick. 'Busy times… I just popped by to tell you I think you'd better go upstairs.'

'Easier said than done,' I grumble.

'True,' he says, 'but think of me after the accident. As soon as I was able to walk more than a few steps, I'd climb the hills behind my house to see the Montagues and Capulets every day, dragging this,' he slaps his lame leg, 'behind me.'

'I know, I know,' I say, although actually this historical detail is a sore point. A heartbroken Luigi toiling up the misty hill towards those two towers had been the opening scene of the screenplay I'd written about him: *The Verona Diaries*. It was turned down flat by nineteen production companies.

'All I'm saying is, if an old invalid like me can do it, you can make it up a couple of flights.'

I feel another swell of annoyance. But before I can sound off at another 'mind over matter' pep talk, he puts his hands up in resignation and walks off down the stairs of the bedroom without a word, leaving just the cushion at the back of the armchair, squashed with the imprint of his backside.

Whitney Houston's bowl turns out to be surprisingly difficult to carry. I stagger from one end of my bed to the other. It's been a while since anyone changed Whitney's water and it looks gloomy. A ring of green algae rocks about the perimeter as I try to manoeuvre it. By the time

I manage to position it (just below Max's pillow where it can catch two sets of drips at once), I'm exhausted, lonely and suddenly furious at his absence.

I walk down the mezzanine steps, punching out a new message. *Venturing out. I may be some time.*

6

Landing

I press the bell by Mrs Rothwell's front door and sag against the wall.

Sudden darkness. The hallway light has timed out again.

'Well done, *cara mia*,' whispers Luigi from somewhere close by. 'No mean feat to make it up those stairs. I'm proud of you. Exercise, if carefully paced, is a crucial part of the road to recovery. I may have a limp, but I'm pretty strong these days. Particularly my core. Look, I'll tense, and you can punch me here…'

'Right,' I murmur, wondering if it's obligatory to become self-obsessed in order to be 'released'. 'Maybe later.'

I reach around the wall, feeling for a switch like I am trying to read Braille, when I have a sudden feeling of extreme light-headedness.

Then darkness again, but this time it is complete.

*

The next thing I know, I'm lying on my side with that particular nerve-jangling pain of a banged elbow and feeling the roughness of worn carpet under my cheek. Above me, a silhouette in a doorway. The hallway light snaps on.

I swivel my head, too fast. Feel a flash of carpet burn along my jaw. Dizziness sparks behind my eyes.

Then I'm staring up at the familiar figure of Danny Cousins.

He stoops down to examine me, his face so close that it's out of focus. For some reason he's wearing an enormous pair of headphones, the old-fashioned kind that pilots use.

'Danny?' I croak, my mouth a desert. So he did get the email. 'How the hell…'

'Don't try to talk. You may have broken something. Going to roll you onto your side, then sit you up if you think you can manage? Good.' Gentle but firm hands are rolling me off my back, releasing my elbow from where it's been squashed under my torso. 'Helluva tumble you took. I heard it from my room, even with the headphones on.'

'Why the American accent?' I murmur as he props me up against the wall. 'Doesn't suit you.'

'Not a whole lot I can do about that.'

He rocks back on his heels and the features sharpen. Short dark hair and a few days of beard. Calm, olive-coloured eyes. Strong, peaked eyebrows. Not Danny Cousins.

'Sorry… I… For a moment, you looked just like someone I know.'

'Dispiriting how many people tell me that. I'm going to take a wild guess here – you're the sick girl from the basement?'

Am I delirious? Still in The Pit? It's true he does look a bit like Danny, but it's hardly enough for me to mistake him at close quarters. This man's face is quite different, despite the beard. And although he's the same sort of size as Danny, with the same broad shoulders and wide face, he doesn't seem to take up space in the same way. For a well-built man there's something modest about his presence.

He straightens up. 'I'll get you some sugary tea.'

'No,' I say, a little too emphatically. 'No need. I'll just take a minute.'

'Everyone needs sugary tea,' he says. 'It's the only medicine that really works.'

'I don't want it.'

'Sure you do.'

And without waiting for an answer, he walks back into the apartment, leaving the door swinging open.

'You have to admit *that*…' says Luigi, puffing up the stairs '… is quite uncanny.'

'You see it too?'

'Very strong resemblance.'

'Thank God.' I breathe out again. 'For a moment, I thought I was going mad.'

'It's not just physical,' says Luigi, leaning against the wall and resting his bad foot behind him. 'Something else, too.'

'Please don't be cryptic.'

'Haven't put my finger on it either. Yet. I'll watch him closely—'

Footsteps in the hallway.

'Catch you later,' says Luigi, pushing off from the wall and disappearing down the stairs as fast as a lame ghost can go.

'Thanks,' I say, as the man with the American accent hands me a cup of tea. 'Didn't mean to be rude.'

He has a mug for himself as well. To my surprise, he slides down the wall and perches on the top step. He still has the headphones on, but they're slung around his neck like a sports commentator's.

'I didn't take it as rude,' he says, blowing across his tea. 'Kinda charming-rude maybe.'

He's wearing a faded green t-shirt, which either has fashionable external seams or he's got it on inside out. Judging by his face, I'd say the latter, which – although he can only be a few years older than me – has a rugged, lived-in quality. The olive-coloured irises have flecks in them, like splinters in a smashed glass. Yellows, browns and greens. And he has an ear clip, a tiny fold of plain metal on the rim of his left ear.

He looks up and catches me staring.

I drop my eyes, embarrassed, and take a sip of tea. It is sweet and a little smoky.

'You were in the middle of something,' I say, gesturing at the headphones. 'I'm okay now. Really. Don't let me keep you.'

He smiles over his mug. 'Don't worry, this is ideal for me. Procrastinating with an actual excuse. I've been stuck on this commission for six weeks, might as well be forever. I keep blaming the city. All the noise, drowning out the music. But the truth is, my real gift is wasting time wherever I am.'

I'm starting to feel a little better. Perhaps he's right and it's the sugar. Strength returning slowly, the stuffing being packed back into the scarecrow. I feel the fog clearing from the corridors of my brain, words reassembling, connecting with their meaning, questions forming. Who is this not-Danny-Cousins person who was busy working on something upstairs in the old lady's flat. Did he mean *actual* music that was drowned out or was that a figure of speech?

'You're in good company,' I tell him. 'I've sunk a lot of time into old movies and crosswords over the years.'

'Snap,' says the man. 'Which crosswords do you do? I've been losing heart with *The Times* recently, they all seemed so formulaic, then the other day I came across this *beautiful* clue...'

It sounds so like something Gracie would say that I feel a sharp sense of disbelief, remembering the gap between us. *Enough's enough*, I think. *Let's make up.*

While we talk, he fiddles with the buckle of a chainmail watch that he wears loose around his wrist, like a bracelet.

'I had a boyfriend who was even better at procrastinating than me,' I say. 'He told me I was his muse, which I loved of course. It took me a while to realise that I was actually his excuse for not doing much at all.'

'A muse?' He smiles, and I'm surprised to see his teeth are very white and straight. 'Good line though.'

'Isn't it? There might have been a germ of truth there. I think creatives only really write for one person. The trick is working out who.'

His face changes at this. Just for a moment. The playful look slipping; something else behind it. Then the smile comes back again. Click-clack goes the watch buckle.

We sit in easy silence for a while.

'You know, you should collapse on our landing more often.'

'You're right. I don't know why – oh, my *god*! The flood!'

He lifts an eyebrow.

'Really. I'm not joking. A lot of water. Coming from your bathroom, into our bedroom.' I stand up so quickly that sparks flash in front of my eyes again. 'You need to hurry. I've left Whitney Houston on the bed…'

'Wait!' He stands up too, puts out a hand. 'Hold up. Whitney *Houston*?'

'Name of my goldfish.'

'Got it.' He nods, deadpan. 'You better come inside while I check. You're in no state to do the stairs right now. Deal?' He holds my eye until I nod.

He lends a steadying arm and I take a few steps forward, over the threshold.

And all of a sudden, I'm somewhere else. Another floor in the same building, with the same footprint as ours, but it may as well be another world.

I put my hand out to touch the wall. This time, less for balance than to check that it's really there.

7

Upstairs

I grew up in a house where everything was painted white and came in pairs. One summer holiday, when I must have been about eight, Faye asked me to train our two white greyhounds to sit either side of the front doorstep. She measured with a ruler and marked a cross on each side, so that the marks were equidistant from the edges. I had to give them treats when they sat down exactly in their positions. She wanted to train our dogs to be symmetrical ornaments. That seemed normal then.

These days I can only truly relax in spaces full of colourful clutter, with no undercurrent of control.

So Mrs Rothwell's living room – which would have given Faye angina – was an oasis to me. The curtains, printed with large blown roses, are half-drawn, as if someone had been distracted mid-task. Most of the room is lined with sagging bookshelves, stacked both ways to cram in as many titles as possible. The remaining wall space is teeming with pictures that have no apparent governing principle: tiny oil paintings of nudes; posters advertising rock concerts; photos of food-markets, underwater coral gardens, suspension bridges. On a side-table by the window is a glass box showcasing a large, stuffed rodent with comically big front teeth – is it a beaver? A marmot? – standing up on its hind legs with one paw urgently raised, apparently hailing a cab.

It takes me a few moments to spot the piano that's been the soundtrack of my last few months. It's partially screened from where I'm sitting by a ferocious-looking pot-plant and a battered wingback armchair: an ebony upright, lid closed and piled high with more books, a messy stack of sheet music and a modern clip-on desk lamp, which has been angled to illuminate the music stand.

I sink into the sofa, feeling the aches from my short trip to The Pit recede. It still doesn't feel real to me that I made it up here. I find myself hoping:

a. Max hasn't come home to find a bath in the bed;
b. Whitney Houston isn't under it;
c. I find out more about the time-wasting American…

when Mrs Rothwell appears in the doorway, brandishing a large vape.

She is younger than I'd imagined. Perhaps not even seventy. Smaller too, wrapped up in a patterned silk Japanese dressing gown. She has short, mid-brown hair, a beaky nose, and a bright gaze that is now studying me with interest.

'So you made it to the summit,' she says in an amused, gravelly voice that suggests decades of late nights, smoking and sordid fun. 'Jesse and I have been taking bets as to whether you actually exist.'

Jesse. The American. Suits him.

'I've been wondering that a lot lately myself.'

'But as you do exist, I'm sorry to hear we made a mess of your ceiling.'

She flashes me a smile and, lips knitting together with purpose, walks over to the armchair by the piano. I revise her age upwards by a good five years. She has one of those slow, stiff gaits that makes her thin frame suddenly look frail rather than wiry.

'Even more sorry to hear you are unwell,' she says as she lowers herself carefully using both armrests. She sits back, cheeks tinged by the exertion, and takes a long pull on the vape. 'I assume you can't drink in your condition?' She leans to one side of her chair, left sleeve billowing, and opens the door to a small dark-wood Chinese cabinet. 'A flood plus a visitor seems like the perfect excuse for a whisky.'

She puts a bottle and two tumblers on the coffee table and starts unscrewing the cap like she means business.

‘Would I be *very* irresponsible to offer you one?’

I hesitate. Since I’ve been ill, I have tried alcohol once, in desperation. A shot of vodka in the middle of the day, to see what would happen. I was fine when I drank it, but my next visit to The Pit was particularly extended and vicious.

‘Very,’ I confirm, sticking out a hand for the tumbler.

She smiles and sloshes in three fingers. A powerful woody smell fills the room. ‘This may sound very tactless but I can’t tell you how exciting it is to have a visitor. Since Jesse moved back in, we see no one apart from my pupils.’

‘So Jesse is your…’

I leave the sentence hanging.

She doesn’t pick it up.

‘… tenant?’ I’m forced to add, awkwardly.

‘Friend,’ she corrects tersely, like she’s shutting a box.

Then she leans forward, her gaze suddenly intent. ‘Right. So tell me. How long have you been this way? All I’ve heard is you’ve been ill for months. I want to know everything.’

To my embarrassment, I feel tears shoot to my eyes. I blink them back, concentrate on the whisky burn on my lips.

‘When you say “everything”?’

She waves her vape, unsmiling. ‘All of it. As much as you can bear.’

*

Most people, even the ones who love you, are weird around sickness. Take my old friend Jenny. If you're on the phone with her and mention you're feeling a bit fluey, she'll clam up and find an excuse to dump the call right away; like her 'battery is dying' or she's about to drive into a tunnel. Sometimes, uncannily, both at the same time. I can't exactly *prove* that Jenny's fearful she'll pick up germs through the phone line, that even talking to a sick person will mean something mucousy will rub off on her. But if you meet her in person and tell her about someone you know who is sick, she'll pull her sweater up over her mouth and start wheezing at you like she's Darth Vader.

Jenny may be a germaphobe, and superstitious to boot, but there's a range of solid reasons people don't like the sick: they're boring and they smell and they're far too eager to dish out their sick-bed epiphanies. Chronic sickness is much worse. Something about the fact that you are stuck, that you can't deliver the reassuring narrative of 'getting better', feels unnatural, disturbing. Worse, in some ways, than death. Death is unimaginable and your brain stalls at the concept. Whereas long-term sickness is claustrophobic and terrifying, but somehow familiar. Like that very specific feeling when an Underground train grinds to a halt in a tunnel and the lights start to flicker.

So when this salty old woman who lives in chaos with a stuffed marmot leans in right away – not just asking but *demanding* to know all about it – something inside me shifts. Perhaps it's the exhilaration of making it out the flat unaided, perhaps it's the whisky (most definitely the whisky). But for the first time since it started, the whole story comes tumbling out: the brief initial sickness, the jagged descent, the misplaced optimism around recovery, the slow dawning that things were not improving at all, followed by the weeks of tedium and terror.

Mrs Rothwell listens carefully. Now and then she disappears behind a new cloud of smoke or prompts me with an astute question. For the first few minutes I keep up my usual lighthouse sweep for any trace of scepticism or boredom in her expression. It's what stopped me wanting visitors after the first few weeks, either family (the hardest) or eventually friends. I'd find myself more depleted after they came, partly from the energy expended in actual conversation – sometimes the muscles in my face seemed to rebel against forming words – but also because I couldn't bear what I saw in their eyes. The more they tried to hide it, the more it cost me. Pity and doubt, draining me like vampires.

But bit by bit, it dawns on me that there is neither here. And this sensation of being listened to without judgement is so new, but also such a profound relief, that when she says 'So what's it like down there in The Pit?', I pause, but don't shut her down completely like I did the others.

'Hard to describe.'

'Try.'

‘Really, it’s so weird down there—’

‘I like weird,’ she says, in a way that makes me believe her. ‘What have you got to lose? Close your eyes and pretend I’m not here. Then describe what it’s like, as if you’re talking to yourself.’

I close my eyes.

I see it like an inverted volcano, I tell her.

To start with there’s the Pain. That’s the top rung. It can be fierce, or dull, or swing between the two. It can catch you off guard, which makes the fear flare. But for the most part, you can get used to it fairly quickly. After the initial panic – *I’m not better, it’s coming back* – you remind yourself you are lying on a bed with clean sheets, with a goldfish swimming beside you, with no terminal illness and all your limbs attached, and you shut the fuck up. A physical endurance test. No less, no more.

Next (in descending order) there’s Loneliness. Not the usual kind, which can be solved by speaking to people. But the kind that makes you wonder if you’ve always been lonely. That makes you question, as the darkness wraps around you, if that essential part within, the far shore against which the sickness wrecks you, has ever been known. Weirdly, you can get used to that part too. A kind of emptiness descends, in which nothing matters, so nothing is lost.

Below, things start to really heat up. Because that’s when The Pit changes; the walls constrict and grow slippery, and the voices swirl and echo around you. The ones who don't believe you. The ones who think it's all in your head. You can stay on that rung for hours, looping round and round, listening to them judging you. Whispering and shooting glances, suspecting you're one of *those* people: a hysteric, looking for attention; or a victim, wanting to duck out of her life.

You think that's the bottom, the place where the voices live, until you fall through the trapdoor into the place that feels most unbearable of all. The smallest and darkest space, where two monsters that should have torn each other to pieces long ago appear to co-exist. The first you meet is a prowling dread that circles your brain again and again, telling you that this is now who you are forever: stuck in bed; in life; in time. One of those people you've pitied from afar but never thought you'd be. And just when that horror feels like it has filled you, the other one shows up. A snapping, snarling shape-shifter. Hot breath, stinking of self-doubt. That tells you that the voices were right all along. That you made it all up. Which makes you the last person you can ever trust.

When I open my eyes, Mrs Rothwell is looking at me steadily.

'How mad did that sound?'

She shakes her head. 'Maddening. Not mad.' And she looks so completely devoid of boredom or distrust, just a quiet kind of interest and something else – something

I haven't seen in anyone's eyes for months. It takes me a few moments to register what this is. Respect. Just then, Jesse walks in, the knees of his jeans wet and damp hair pushed back off his hot face, and I feel a surge of resentment. *Go away,* I think. *I need this space more than you do.*

He seems to sense this and keeps one hand on the door to the living room.

'Hey. Sorry to interrupt, but the leak is fixed,' he says. 'The shower-head was off the cradle and dripping down the side of the bath. Must have been like that for hours. I went through six towels mopping it up.' He wipes his hands on his jeans. 'I left the bath panel off to let in air, but some water has soaked through already.'

Mrs Rothwell winces. 'Oh, hell. Sounds like we owe you a huge apology, Vita.'

'"*We?*" Really?' says Jesse.

'There will be some insurance somewhere,' Mrs Rothwell adds vaguely.

Jesse's gaze falls on the whisky bottle and the tumblers in our hands. I catch him and Mrs Rothwell exchanging glances. For a moment she looks like a naughty schoolgirl, and I wonder again at their relationship. Is he an assistant of some sort? A godson? I feel like he's going to say something provoking, like, *Not exactly what the doctor ordered*, but instead he breaks into that surprisingly beautiful smile.

'You found a kindred spirit, I see,' he says, though it's not clear whether this is directed to Mrs Rothwell or the whisky. 'If you're both okay, I'm going to dive back into work. I had an idea about some phrasing, believe it or not, when I was wringing out the bathmat.'

Lots of things happen on his face at once, I think, stealing another glance. Mischief layered over melancholy, a sad tiredness in his eyes.

'You should grab his autograph while you can,' Mrs Rothwell is saying. 'He's about to become a very famous musician.'

'Don't believe a word.' Jesse shakes his head. 'She's been saying that for years.'

'Would I know any of your work?' I ask.

He flinches. 'Doubt it.'

'Definitely,' says Mrs Rothwell.

They both look at each other.

She describes a Christmas advert for a famous department store, which I remember flooding the commercial breaks last year. 'Right now he's writing the title music for this big sci-fi series on TV with whatsherface. Emily thingy.'

I glance over at Jesse. 'Aha. Emily thingy, is it?'

'If I finish it before setting fire to myself. Anyway,' he fiddles with his watch again, 'back to the computer. I just came by to—'

'Such a shame the way people make music now,' says Mrs Rothwell, knocking back the last of her whisky. 'Sealed off from any audience, staring at a screen so they can't *feel* how other people hear it. He plays the guitar so beautifully, you know. The piano, too.'

'Well, *he* is off now,' says Jesse, rocking the door back and forth. He makes to go, then turns back. That smile again. At me, this time. 'Unless you need a hand getting downstairs?'

I look at him blankly.

'Now everything's fixed.'

'Oh, yes,' I say, half-rising in confusion. Of course, I should leave now, Mrs Rothwell is in her dressing gown so was probably in bed when I arrived. It occurs to me while I've been feeling understood and seen for the first time in months, she's been babysitting the mad, sick girlfriend of the nice doctor from downstairs. They both have.

'Like hell she's going,' says Mrs Rothwell, putting out a restraining hand. 'We're just getting into it.' She looks at me. 'I'm an old bat and don't sleep at night. Presumably you sleep all day? It's the perfect time for us to get to know each other.'

Jesse looks strangely pleased about this. 'Well, if you're both okay.'

'Thank you,' I say, my face heating up. 'It was nice of you to... procrastinate with me.'

He gives me a mock salute. 'Any excuse.'

He's still smiling as he turns away. From the corner of my eye, I can feel Mrs Rothwell watching both of us. She looks down, humming, and starts refilling her vape.

To hide my awkwardness, I turn to the cluster of photos on the side-table next to me. Many of them are of one particular man: older but still very handsome, hair and eyebrows greying, then grey. In one of them he is sitting, legs dangling, on the edge of a stage, holding a guitar. In another he is laughing while smoking what appears to be a very large joint.

I pick up the smallest frame, the size of a playing card, which shows him, young and lean, with a youthful, long-haired, fuller-cheeked Mrs Rothwell, lying in some long grass. He's reading and she's sketching, her back propped against his bent knees for support. They could pass for film stars, I think, and there is something about his hand loosely draped along her side that touches me profoundly.

'That's Col,' says Mrs Rothwell. 'Always took his shirt off at the drop of a hat, the dreadful poser.'

I register the past tense. That's right. Max had said she'd lost her husband recently.

She reads the pause between us.

'One year, one month and four days ago,' she says.

'I'm so sorry.'

She nods. 'He was in a band, too. Not that he made any money from it. He was a primary school teacher first and foremost. But we were a musical family. That's why Jesse first moved in as a—' She pauses.

I wait for her to finish, but she doesn't.

'It's a wonderful photo,' I say, meaning it.

Her face relaxes. 'Isn't it? The first time I met Col was at a friend's house. I woke up and heard someone playing the guitar downstairs. Fifties blues and jazz stuff. Ray Charles. Not normally my thing. But I walk in and there he is, totally absorbed. This beautiful black man, eyes closed, with a rapt expression on his face. Doesn't even notice me coming in. I sit on a window seat at the back of the room, listening. At the time I had a boyfriend I was losing interest in, though I didn't know it until then. And I remember so clearly thinking to myself: *That's what I want. A man who can hear the music…*' She trails off, touching her cheek as if it is someone else's. 'And that's what I got. Col could be a pain in the arse, but he heard the music all the time.' For a moment or two the expression on her face is so private, so passionate, so completely unexpected on a woman of her age, with her wrinkled face and beaky nose, that, moved and embarrassed, I look down at my empty whisky glass.

'I have a burst of energy now,' I say, patting the arm of the sofa. 'I should really go. While the going is good.'

'I'll allow it,' says Mrs Rothwell, getting up too. She begins her stiff walk to the door. 'As long as next time you have a burst, you come up again. I have many more questions.'

It's not until I'm on my feet that I realise I am still holding the small wrought-iron-framed photo of the Rothwells. I'm about to place it back amongst the crowd of other frames when I have a sudden sensation of Luigi being in the room somewhere. I hear his voice.

Rule-breakers like you and me…

I close my hand around the metal and slide it into my pocket.

8

Roots

By the time I make it back to my bed, lug Whitney's bowl off the mattress, strip off the top sheet and crawl under the covers, I can feel the dark pull of The Pit again. That tingling in my fingers and toes, and soon after a crushing mix of weakness and heaviness in my legs followed by the long suck downwards. I'm assailed by a sudden, fierce longing to see Gracie, to tell her that I made it upstairs alone for the first time in months, that perhaps Luigi really is releasing me. I count the weeks since I last saw her. It's funny, but all I can think of is that by now she'll be needing her roots done.

I dip the brush back into the bowl of dye and carefully wipe the dribbles off.

'Hold still, will you?' I say, with an edge to my voice. 'I can't do it properly if you keep throwing your head around like a racehorse.'

It's been a couple of hours since she tickled my arm. Neither of us has brought up Max or the argument since. In the space between us the truce is fragile.

I'm kneeling behind her on the bed, wearing thin rubber gloves that make my fingers whisper and squeak. She has a dark towel around her shoulders and has combed out her wet, pink hair so that I can see the two inches of offending brown grading into the magenta.

'In other words, button the fuck up,' says Gracie cheerfully. *Which, let's face it, has always been your modus operandi.* She doesn't say the second part, but the words hang in the air between us just as surely as if she had, and I wonder whether it will always be like this, the love and guilt and judgement and betrayal fighting for space, elbowing each other out the way.

She's relaying some awful story from twenty years ago about Dad and Faye in the car on the M40 on the way to a waterpark near Oxford. I'm half-listening, focused on dabbing the dye on small sections then pulling the hair neatly over like I've seen them do in salons. Perhaps I occasionally give the roots more of a yank than I need to.

I'm loading up with more dye when I hear Gracie saying, 'Which means Dad was fucking someone right under Faye's nose.'

My brush freezes mid-air. 'Wait. *What?*'

Gracie twists round, holding her towel close to her neck. She takes one look at my face and snorts. 'When did you stop listening?'

I hesitate. 'I don't know… Around the petrol station?'

Gracie snorts. ''Course you did. That's why you remember nothing. According to you, our childhood is a *tabula rasa*.'

I grit my teeth. 'Why can't you say blank slate like everyone else?'

I start dabbing again, making the movements as quick and rhythmic as I can, resisting an urge just to slosh the dye all over.

As it happens, I do remember. It was the ninth of August 2003 or 2004. Gracie's tenth or eleventh birthday, not sure which. One of those boiling English days that you wait for all year, but when it happens leaves you feeling breathless and overpowered. It had been Faye's idea to go to the waterpark. When Dad told me I didn't push back, despite knowing Gracie hated rides, especially ones involving water. So, we waited in the long, sticky queue for the Log Flume, while my father and Faye stood in the shade by the refreshments van. Faye was wearing this hat, beige and black straw with a very wide rim. And Gracie's hand got damper and tighter in mine as the queue moved forward. 'I don't want to do it,' she kept whispering. 'I don't want to.' I squeezed her hand back and told her that it would be fun, that she should remember what Faye said in the car ride there about the entrance fees being a fortune and people travelling from all over the country just to come here. Then we were on the steps leading up to the top of the plastic mountain where the Log Flume began, and Faye's hat was getting smaller and smaller in the crowd. Gracie was really pulling back now, trying to resist the push of the people behind us. 'Please don't make me, Vee,' she kept saying, tugging at my hand. '*Please* don't make me.'

And then suddenly we're on the ride and she's sitting behind me, sobbing and sobbing, her small hands clutching the back of my shirt as the carriage shoots down the track, water sheeting out and drenching us. When we reach the bottom Gracie is crying so hard she can't climb out. Won't budge, even when I plead and try to drag her. Which is when Faye shows up, spitting poison. Gracie is still sitting there, sodden and shivering like she's on another planet. But as soon as she sees Faye, she stands up like a robot and steps out onto the platform. I get a glimpse of her face, sheet-white and broken. Then the shame and fear in the outline of her little body as Dad marches her to the car park.

'So at some point Dad takes me back to the Volvo,' says Gracie, 'because I'd pulled a whitey on a ride – I can't really remember that bit but I wonder now whether it was a precursor to my fits. He's telling me that Faye finds me impossible, that I should try and behave more like you… all the usual horseshit… when his phone rings. So he gets out of the car to answer it.'

The problem was he'd left the car window open, says Gracie. So although he was a few metres away, back turned, she could hear the whole thing. Maybe he thought ten-year-olds didn't understand anything like that. Or maybe, in his passion, he thought he was talking more in code than he was.

'Well, go *on,*' I say, feeling a bit like you do when you pass a pile-up on the motorway. Fascinated, despite myself.

'Some of it's fuzzy,' says Gracie. 'It's hard to know exactly what's memory and what I've embroidered over the years. Maybe I'm wrong about all the "I love yous" and "darlings". The only bit I'd swear by – and it's crystal-clear in my memory because it was the word that shocked me – was when Dad lowered his voice and said, "You're all I think about when I'm with my family. It's driving me to distraction. I just want to be fucking you all the time."'

My mouth falls open. 'Bullshit!'

'I know, right?'

Dye drips off the brush.

'*Dad* said that?'

'I know.'

I can feel Gracie has turned to watch my face as I kneel there, silent and astounded. Trying to imagine our father in love with another woman. Our father, who loves colour but agreed to have the whole house painted white, who hates spicy food but eats curries three times a week, who allowed Faye to knock our old bedrooms together so that Magnus could have a huge one to himself, who lives with cats he's allergic to and votes for who she tells him to and has dropped all of his old friends, let her separate them from him, one after another, like she was slowly peeling off a glove, finger by finger. Our father, who spends his life running around after his second wife, obsessed with fulfilling her every wish, caving to every unreasonable and demeaning demand. Who let our mother be erased. Who looked the other way and chose Faye over us, again and again.

'I should have told you,' says Gracie. 'I'm sorry. I think I always felt guilty for eavesdropping on something I knew I shouldn't have.'

I shake my head. 'God, I hope so.'

It takes her a moment. Then her expression changes. 'Oh, me too,' she breathes. 'I hope he was shagging some hottie who could twist herself into a pretzel in bed.'

'I hope he was fucking her on all those work trips,' I agree.

'In planes.'

'In trains.'

'In glass elevators.'

And we both start laughing so hard that before long there are magenta tears running down Gracie's jaw, and for a moment, just for a moment, it's like they're washing the past clean away.

9

Leap of Faith

The mattress rocks as he changes position. Max often has difficulty sleeping, especially after he's been operating. He uses the phrase 'tired and wired' rather than 'insomnia' or 'trauma'. But I often wonder about what effect it has, neurologically, to slice people open almost daily. Or partly disembowel them, rearranging the heavy coils of gut like pipework in a bloody basement.

I look up at the ceiling. A large proportion of it is stained the colour of weak tea, but it doesn't look as bad in the daylight, no broken paintwork or blistering. I reach over for my phone, feeling weak but not drastically so. Some warning numbness at the tips of my fingers – *you're reaching the edge of your energy envelope* – but I seem to have got away with the whisky from yesterday.

A few minutes past ten in the morning. I must have conked out after all.

I open my mail app and refresh it.

One from Tom, my boss, which I read with a sigh: he's come up with a new list of interviewees for the podcast; 'no pressure, obvs' but he thinks I may want to cast my eye over it. A few circulars, stuff I always mean to unsubscribe from. Nothing interesting.

'Tell me it's Thursday,' Max mumbles without opening his eyes.

'It's Thursday.'

He puts out an arm, reaching for me. 'Thank fuck.'

'When do you need to go in?'

'Midday. God, that was a long night. I fell asleep on the bus.'

'You didn't get my messages then? About the flood.'

'What mess… oh, shit,' says Max, sitting up suddenly. He pushes back the covers, reaching for his glasses. 'I assumed you were winding me up.' He climbs on the bed to take a closer look overhead. 'Christ.' He presses the stain on the ceiling gingerly, like it's a bruise. 'Has it definitely stopped? We're going to need to tell Mrs Rothwell and the American guy who lives with her…'

'Jesse. I already did. Actually, he's a—'

'They came down?'

'No. I went up.'

Max looks at me so suddenly that his glasses slide down his nose. Then drops into a sitting position next to me. 'You went up the stairs alone?'

I nod.

'Vita Meredith Woods,' he says, leaning in to kiss me. 'You are…'

'Don't say *getting better*,' I pull back with a warning note in my voice. 'Because maybe tomorrow will be shit again. And then—'

'… the most courageous, unpredictable and exciting person I know,' he says. 'When's the date?'

'The date?' I echo.

'Yes, Ms Woods, the date.' He winces and rubs his shoulder. 'For our next leap of faith.'

I laugh. 'Sure you want to risk it?'

The first was two weeks after I moved into Alvanley Gardens. Max had gone to the hardware store for some bits and pieces. I'd been under the duvet all day, not sick just yet but hit by a paralysing sadness, the kind of stiff-faced, dry-eyed depression that feels like your whole body is in revolt against the fact of life. Then Max walked into the flat, and in the strained voice of someone carrying something heavy, called up for me to: 'Say hello to the Queen of R&B.'

I looked through the mezzanine railings in time to see him staggering into the kitchen and heaving a goldfish bowl onto the table. The sun was slanting through the glass garden door and I remember that first aerial view so well: a fiery little bulb sloshing about amidst plastic seaweed and fish furniture, the fronds of her translucent tail floating behind her.

'Our first pet,' Max said, grinning up at me. 'I thought we could name her Whitney Houston. After your sister's deplorable taste in music.'

I burst into tears, then. A sudden release that racked through me like a coughing fit and subsided, a few minutes later, in a wave of elation. And that's when, still leaning over the handrail, I asked Max to marry me.

At first, he went red-eared with shock. He'd been dropping hints recently, trying to gauge whether I was ready, so I knew he was on the brink. I could see that this new, unscheduled turn of events – Juliet leaning over the balcony and hitting on Romeo – derailed him completely.

A brief but deafening silence.

Then he smiled and held out his arms to me. 'Jump!'

'You're joking.'

He planted his feet, stretched his arms wider. 'Come on, then. I'm ready.'

I scrambled one leg over the railing and looked down. It was further than I thought.

'If this is some kind of trust test…' I muttered.

'Don't think! I'll catch you.'

'Promise?'

'Promise.'

Which to be fair, he did – right before he collapsed under my weight and dislocated his shoulder.

*

After news of my journey upstairs, Max goes to take a shower and make breakfast. As soon as he is out of sight, I open the drawer of the bedside table and take out the photograph of the Rothwells.

'Love the fact that you swiped that,' says Luigi from the end of the bed. He's not wearing his usual garb, but instead is wrapped in a freshly laundered waffle-weave dressing-gown.

I crane down the stairs to check that the shower is still on. 'You think?' I say, looking back at the photo in my hand. 'I'm not even sure why I did it.'

'Quite obvious to me,' says Luigi, glancing at his reflection in the window and patting down a lock of hair that is sticking up from the rest. 'It was very beautiful, the way she talked about her husband. Those things are rare.' He looks wistful for a moment. 'When you come across it, you want to stay close.'

I gaze at him, wondering if this is true.

My phone pings. A text from someone not in my contacts.

Say nothing to annoy royal who neglects duties? (7)

Second letter H.

A little lurch in my stomach. I feel my cheeks go hot.

'What's that?'

'Just a crossword clue.'

Luigi's eyebrows shoot up. 'From himself upstairs? Well, well.'

'Don't know how he got my number,' I mumble.

'Do you know what it is?'

'What what is?'

'The *answer*, of course.'

I study it for a couple more minutes. It's been months since I did my last crossword – five and a half months in fact – but this is not a hard one. *Say nothing...* possibly 'SH'. Royal. CR? ER? I start laughing as soon as I work it out. How on earth had he laid his hands on this? Had he made it up? 'Yes,' I say. 'I know the answer.'

'Do you really?' Luigi looks excited. 'Well, get a move on. The quicker you text back, the more impressed he'll be.'

I type back: *Shirker*.

The phone pings almost immediately.

Takes one to know one.

I chew my nail, to stop myself grinning.

'Oh, my,' says Luigi, fanning his face with one hand.

Another ping.

How's the ceiling? And you?

A noise downstairs. 'Do you know where my razor is?' shouts up Max.

It takes me a moment.

'Behind the shower gel,' I yell back. 'Might have blunted the blade. Sorry!'

'Don't be,' his voice floats up. 'Got some more yesterday.' He's being generous, but the homey chat unsettles me: how did things get so domestic, so fast?

*

Saturday morning, a little over a year ago. In fact, I know the date: 21 August.

I'd taken an unwise turn on the drive home from the shops and run into a market in full swing. London was having one of those summer mornings that felt like we'd stolen it from Europe; everyone was out, tourists in flip-flops walking slowly past stalls, the smell of deep-fried falafel and garlic, a bin lorry beeping pointlessly because there was no space to reverse.

Aside from a mild hangover and the traffic, I was in rip-roaring spirits. I'd told Gracie weeks ago that I'd picked up wetsuits for her and me, then forgotten actually to do it. So I left her sleeping on the inflatable mattress in my flat and snuck off with her car on the off chance the camping shop on the edge of the market might have some surf gear. There, waiting for me on the rack, were two all-weather wetsuits – a size S and an XS – both fifty percent off in the end-of-summer sale. On the street outside, a woman with a tattoo of barbed wire, roses and hearts wrapped around her neck, was standing behind a table selling sunglasses, so I bought myself a pair of giant white sixties-style glasses and some cheap Aviators for Gracie.

All of which was to say, life was good because I was off to Cornwall for a week with my sister.

It was the first holiday we'd taken together for a couple of years; a coincidence not normally afforded by my job (says Gracie), or the state of her body or mind (says me). But it had been a while now since her last 'event', as she liked to refer to her epilepsy. She'd packed up the endless weed-smoking, which could make even her obvious and repetitive and, hallelujah, she'd dumped Dave, the unemployed ayahuasca teacher from Worthing. Although I felt slightly nervous about how the dynamic would play out – five days and nights in a tent is a long time to spend with another person, especially if they're Gracie – I was also longing for this time together in a way that felt close to romantic love.

Because there is no one better in the world to travel with than Gracie. Something about her complete open-mindedness to how the day plays out, and the way she can strike up conversations with unlikely locals who'll end up showing her some secret corner of their lives ('Do you want to meet my bees?'), means that you never end up feeling like a tourist when you're with her. But like you are breaking ground, somehow, outside and in.

In other words, the perfect antidote to the creeping sense of emptiness I felt about my life in London. An emptiness I couldn't quite put my finger on, because even from the inside everything seemed to be thriving. The podcast I worked for, *Confessions*, was going gangbusters. I'd just been promoted to co-producer, and we had a juicy list of future interviewees. And although it was true that I'd more or less given up on my hopes of being a writer, my flat was draughty and I had more clothes on the floor than in the cupboards, at twenty-nine years old I was having fun and managing to pay my way in one of the world's great cities.

It's hard to remember exactly what happened next. Perhaps it's just difficult to separate what happened from what I later told the insurance people. But I do know I had an iced coffee for Gracie in my lap and another cup in my hand when I swung into what might have been a suave one-handed U-turn.

Except it wasn't.

A flash of yellow, then a loud crunch. I was slammed back into the driver's seat and bit down hard on my tongue, coffee spilling through my jean shorts and running down my legs. After I sat there stunned for a moment, I was surprised to find I wasn't really hurt at all. In front of me, there was a bright yellow campervan, one of those old VWs you see at music festivals at this time of year, with ethnic rugs out the back and a Ganesh on the dashboard. I remember thinking that Gracie was going to love this. Proof, as she'd see it, that I've always been the accident waiting to happen, not her.

The driver stepped out of the van, and, with a glance at the front of Gracie's car, was now sitting on his heels inspecting his side door. I stepped out to join him. Closer up, the side of his van looked even worse. There was a concave dent so large it had buckled almost every panel from front to back. Gracie's fender, on the other hand, looked pristine.

'Oh, God, I'm so sorry…' I started to say.

The driver straightened and broke into an easy smile.

'Don't be,' he said. 'It's all mendable.'

He was maybe a couple of years older than me, medium height, dark brown hair, the kind of skin that tans, and dimples in the wrong places, like they'd slipped down to frame his chin. 'I'm Max. You must be Jackie Onassis.'

The sunglasses. I whipped them off, and for some reason – perhaps because the price tag was still dangling – hid them behind my back.

'Sorry,' I said again. 'Have I just wrecked your week-end? Were you headed somewhere fun?'

He rubbed a hand over the stubbled chin. 'If only. On my way back from A and E actually.'

My face must have said 'Oh, shit', because he shook his head and smiled again. 'A cheap shot. I work there. Speaking of which, you okay? Looks like you've bitten your tongue.'

I touched my fingers to my lips and realised my tongue was bleeding. 'I wish I could say it was a first.'

He nodded, as if he understood perfectly. Although he didn't look like the kind of person who ever had to bite his tongue. Clear, brown eyes despite some equally clear traces of tiredness. Confident, I thought. No, better: centred.

'Look, I'm afraid I'm going to have to ask for your details and stuff.'

Insurance. Fuck. We'd always talked about Gracie putting me on her policy, but given the fact that we lived in two different cities, never quite got round to it.

A car honked, then another in quick succession. We had stopped the traffic in both directions.

I hit on a brilliant plan.

'Gracie Woods,' I said, quickly. 'Sorry to meet you this way.'

Max glanced over at a cafe just behind us. 'Listen, Gracie, shall we do this over coffee? I could really do with one. And looks like you need a couple of refills.'

And that's how I met Max, thirteen months ago.

We had our first discussion over cinnamon whirls, about how he was secretly pleased I drove into him, because now he got to change the paint colour of his van, which he'd bought to use for his climbing trips and had seemed, at the time, the perfect antidote to the seriousness of his job. But when you fall out with yellow, you really fall out with it, and what did I think of silver, was that flashy or just a nice change from driving a custard tart? He told me about the long shift he'd just finished, which was filled with all the tragedy and comedy of being a colon surgeon: things being stuck up and rammed down tubes (an umbrella up, a biro down), and at the last moment, a long-standing cancer patient being rushed into ICU with an internal bleed.

It was only four weeks later, after several more of what he pretended were 'meetings' to fill out insurance forms, that I came clean. I told him my name wasn't Gracie, but Vita. By then, of course, he'd already worked that out and was amusing himself by seeing how long it would take me to 'fess up.

The strangest thing about this illness is that it has a tell. The tip of the little finger on my right hand prickles, then goes numb. It's a warning sign, a shot across the bow: you're about to be invaded. After that it starts to colonise limb by limb. Usually it's the legs first (gripping aches); the chest (someone has dumped a pile of bricks on it); the head (squeezing, pulsing, driving – take your pick); blurred vision, stiff joints; the days and nights of draining sleep when you wake feeling like your blood has been flushed through with dirty water and you can't remember your own name. All of which leads you into the labyrinth that takes you from one medical waiting room to the next.

White-coat count, so far: GP (high inflammation markers, but, hmmm, low white blood cells); haematologist (neutrophils very low, we should consider bone-marrow test); oncologist (strange variation in your blood tests, let's keep an eye on it); urologist (all this suggests a compromised immune system); endocrinologist (did your mother have a very early menopause? Ah, sorry for your loss); physician (all points to Mast Cell Activation Syndrome, you need a trio of antihistamines plus wildly expensive, hard-to-source diet); NHS hotline (paracetamol every six hours); ME/Chronic Fatigue/Lyme disease specialist (read my book: *It's Not Hypochondria, It's Mitochondria*). Funny that when the doctors couldn't nail down a diagnosis and I got tired of being ping-ponged between them, I stopped wanting visitors either. I didn't have anything to tell them.

While Max is clattering about in the kitchen, my little finger starts to fizz.

I find myself staring at the potted orchids next to Whitney's bowl, to distract myself. The tallest one is listing to one side in its moss bedding. Its spotted tongue looks like it's trying to lick the glass. Eight orchids, in a fancy china pot – I should have smelled a rat immediately. It's the kind of thing people buy in the first flush of romance. Or on the company credit card when they want something out of you.

'Tom tried to rope me into doing some work today,' I call down, listening to the kettle rattling as it heats up.

'Really? He phoned you?'

'I sent him an email. Thanking him for the orchids. He wrote back seven minutes later, asking if I could manage a briefing call to California.'

I pause, waiting for Max's derision at Tom's calculated 'kindness'.

There's quiet from below.

'So what did you say?'

I frown. 'I said I couldn't, of course. I can't predict when I'll crash, so that's that.'

Another long pause. I sit up, shimmy along the bed; I have a bird's eye view of the kitchen now. Max is crouching down in front of the cupboard, moving things around.

'You think I should have said yes, don't you?'

He doesn't look up. The silence is a beat too long.

I pull hard at the tips of my fingers, one by one, trying to force the blood flow.

I don't know what I find more irritating about Max's deliberate pause. The fact that he has so little understanding of how I'm feeling that he clearly thinks if I give work a go, it will somehow jumpstart my complete recovery (and no doubt, if I went for a run, that would be good for me too). Or that he's too fucking cowardly to say this, but instead will use a patronising silence to invite me to come to that conclusion myself. Worse, *both* things: that he has so little understanding of what's actually happening in my body, but at the same time acts like he's the grown-up, like he's being the sensitive one by not spelling out what he thinks I'd find difficult to hear.

'My love, I can't advise on whether you're up to it,' he says from below. 'Only you can. On the other hand, going up the stairs alone last night, dealing with the flood…'

'I don't want you to *advise* me.'

'But you just asked me to!'

I scrunch and flex my toes, trying to pump the blood back through. If I can fight off the numbness, then sometimes the pain doesn't arrive behind it. Or at least, that's the hope. It's never actually worked out that way.

'I want your understanding, not your advice,' I call down. 'And by the way, you doctors have no business giving any of us advice. Because you don't know what the fuck you're talking about.'

A longer silence. 'You're probably right,' says Max lightly. 'Like I said, only you can know…' he drifts off. '*Rats*, there's no coffee.'

Of course. You better pop to the corner shop, rather than risk thrashing it out.

'I better nip to the corner shop.'

This time it's me that's silent, but he doesn't remark on it.

After he leaves, I email Tom back, telling him I'll do the briefing call with the actor today if they're really stuck, but to make sure it's audio only, please.

By the time I finish typing, the tips of my fingers have gone numb. My muscles are turning to jelly, that strange feeling of something metallic poisoning my blood. If I rest quickly, completely, it may not last for long this time.

I lie back and wait for The Pit to claim me.

10

The Best Angle

I surface to the sound of a voice outside, but not the usual murmur of a snatched conversation and footsteps I often hear floating past on the street. This is just one male voice, sustained, like someone has left the radio on in a parked car.

I wriggle down the bed a little to get the best angle out the half-window. I can see the bottom of Max's jeans and his trainers on the second step, which means he's finishing off a phone call. I can't hear the words exactly, but I can hear the energy shifting around in his voice, which means he's interested, and being interesting, and from time to time he breaks into a guffaw and his trainers lift a bit at the heels as if his whole body is enjoying itself.

I know exactly who he is talking to.

Eventually he walks in and I hear him padding up the stairs.

'Gone cold, I'm afraid,' he says, holding out a coffee.

The air outside has brought new colour to his cheeks. He looks bright-eyed and ridiculously handsome.

I do not say:

That was Izabella on the phone, wasn't it?

How is it possible you took that long to go to the corner shop?

Surely you have enough fucking time to talk in the hospital, you practically live there.

I do:

thank him for the coffee and open the lid to peer inside. He's asked for just the right amount of milk, which means he's been forced to make a fuss, asking the barista for 'just more milk than a flat white and not quite a latte'. He's always thoughtful that way.

While Max is making pancakes, I watch Whitney who is suspended at a forty-five-degree angle in her bowl, sucking at the surface. She does this sometimes and it's disturbing to watch, like I'm witnessing a drowning. I wonder if it's because I don't change her water often enough, or too much, or sometimes (always) forget to add those drops in advance that do something to the chlorine – or then again, maybe *are* chlorine.

'So how is Izabella?' I ask casually, when he arrives up the stairs holding a plate with four neatly rolled-up chocolate pancakes and a couple of napkins.

'Izabella? Why do you ask?'

'Wasn't that who you were talking to on the steps for the last twenty minutes?'

Max grins. 'Spooky how you do that. More like ten. She was just telling me about this new lab where they do quicker turnarounds. It's a little further away, but it might work for the clinic.'

I don't say anything. He sighs. 'Vita, Izabella is a nice person, and a very talented young doctor, and yes, attractive I dare say, but I don't fancy her at all. I think you've seized on the fact that she has an exotic name—'

'Ha! I'm not deranged.' Why *does* she need to spell it with a 'z' anyway? I wonder. Not just because she's from Uruguay. I've looked it up and it's just as pretentious there too.

Max takes a large bite out of his pancake, leaving a perfect dental impression. 'Look, if you feel weird with Izabella coming in on the business, you should say now. She's been great at coming up with ideas, as you know, but no one's made any promises.'

'I don't feel weird.'

'Okay.' He eats his pancake, waiting.

'It's just a bit annoying. That of all people you'd partner up with someone beautiful, brainy and with laidback South American vibes. Not an incredible sense of humour, I've noticed. Not *gripping,* as human beings go, but in all other ways—'

'You know I always follow our rule.'

Our rule. Made up by him. That we should always behave as if the other one of us was in the room. I think about the fact that I'm internet stalking Danny. And now the message from Jesse. If I text back does that constitute being flirty? Am I being particularly twitchy about Izabella because I'm feeling guilty?

Then I feel a wave of crossness. What have I got to feel guilty about? I'm hemmed in enough as it is.

I can feel my feet tingling and starting to lose sensation. I take a couple of deliberate breaths. *Deliberate breathing can have a significant effect on the vagus nerve... To stop your body tipping into fight-or-flight mode, allow it to realise you are not under threat...*

'I'm sorry,' I say. 'Ignore me. I think I'm a bit jangled after last night.'

''Course you are,' says Max. 'Don't apologise.' He reaches for my hands and rubs my fingers, which have turned bluish-white at the tips. 'I just wish I could help more. Some of this microbiome research I'm doing is probably only a handful of years away from understanding the shit you're going through now. That loop between gut and brain and chronic fatigue and how a virus can trip that switch... we're so damn' close! You may feel stuck, but we're the ones playing catch-up.'

He looks at the clock next to Whitney Houston and stands up. 'Is that thing right these days? I'm sorry, honey, I've got to go.'

You've always got to go, I want to say, as the door shuts behind him.

'What about Night Sky?' says Luigi, peering over my shoulder. 'I think Blur looks like you're trying to hide something.'

'Like I'm lying in my sickbed being bossed around by a posh Italian ghost?'

We're trying to find the right background for the video call with the actor in California. Tom had promised me it was audio only – video, I've found, drains me much quicker – but then inevitably sent me a Zoom link twenty minutes beforehand.

I'm worried about crashing and getting stranded in the kitchen, so I've done my best to arrange the quilt and cushions on my bed to make it look like a chaise.

'Seb is just grabbing a shower and will be with you in five.' The blonde PR associate with the skin of a seven-month-old baby is back on the screen. 'So sorry to keep you waiting, Vera.'

'Vita,' I murmur.

Maybe they use the 'touch up my image' option, which would account for the flawless skin. Of course they do, he's a heart-throb in his late forties. Maybe I should, too? I study my face in the digital rectangle. I look thinner, definitely, but not in a good way.

'I'd put your hair down, if I were you,' says Luigi, cocking his head.

'Really?'

I take out the hairband I've been wearing for God knows how many days and my hair slides to one side in a greasy wedge. Luigi shakes his head quickly. Perhaps not. I'm just putting it back up again when Sebastian Rose appears in front of me, in a very low-slung work-out vest. The whites of his eyes and teeth gleam in his tanned face. Not my type. But the familiarity of the famous features still has a strange impact, like whiplash.

'I thought it was the afternoon for you folks over there?' He leans forward, peering into the screen so that his handsome features briefly distort, like he's looking into a fish-eye. 'Did you oversleep or something?'

I glance at the top right of the screen. Seven minutes left. My back is soaked with sweat. My whole job, after this pre-call, is to put together a run of questions so that the interview can sink deep into the 'why' of his behaviour and Salima, the sexy gravel-voiced Greek celebrity psychotherapist who hosts our podcast, can, spontaneously, deliver my poignant conclusion. We're now more than two-thirds of the way through the time I've been given, and he's only served up one mildly negative experience (skiing, broken leg) and nothing remotely resembling a confession.

‘I still don’t understand what I’m supposed to be “confessing” to.’ Sebastian Rose, heart-throb of *The Dark Kingdom* franchise, flashes his perfect gnashers to show me the joke is not on him.

And he’s right. The joke’s not on him. He’s in on the deal. A little bit of intimacy in exchange for a lot of promotion of his current film. With some interviewees, when I get to choose them, I feel like everyone’s getting their money’s worth. Tom’s concept for the show is a good one. A new, more interesting way for celebrities to talk about themselves. A chance to look under the bonnet at a life event that has shaped them. A great way to make a living, I tell my friends. A privilege, really.

Yet two years into producing it, the formula has begun to stick in my throat. The rehearsed ‘authenticity’ of some of the more intelligent stars. The eye-watering entitlement of others. But despite the creeping doubts, it has never felt quite so hollow as it does now, speaking to this vacuous Adonis from my sickbed. Trawling for something to spin into an illusion of substance, some ‘vulnerability’ I can fashion into a trompe l’oeil of intimacy.

‘Oh, I’m sorry. That’s my fault then. Really, it’s just a way of talking about yourself in depth.’ I can hear my voice slurring. My facial muscles have started to numb. I remember that I’m on camera too and resist the urge to slap my own cheeks. 'How difficulties in your past have shaped your future, if you like.'

The handsome brow furrows. Then he breaks into a smile.

'Oh, you should have said! My *trauma*. That's easy...'

11

Ants

It feels like I've just shut my laptop and flopped back on the pillow for a moment when I notice the ants pouring over the edge of my bedside table. They march past the stolen photo of Mr and Mrs Rothwell, then onto the dinner plate where they split and re-form around fragments of remaining pancake. About ten of them are hoisting up a piece that must be the equivalent of ten men carrying a giant marquee. One of them hovers on the outskirts, and from time to time dives in and course-corrects the group. Apart from that you can't tell one from the next. They're all in it together: unified, tireless, ruthless in their focus.

'Don't be too sure about that.'

I look up to see Luigi hovering over me.

'*God*,' I say crossly, because he startled me so much that I spilled my Vitamin C drink. 'Can you try not to shock me like that every time?'

He leans over to watch the stream of ants. 'Everyone talks about what great workers they are, their singularity of purpose. Let me show you what happens when one of them falls behind and holds the others up.'

He crouches down with difficulty and sits back on his heels gasping. Then he reaches out one finger and, with a quick flick, knocks one of the ants onto its back. It lies there, helpless, spindly legs bicycling in the air.

'What did you do that for?'

'Just watch.'

I look on with a sense of trepidation.

There's a moment of confusion as the ones immediately behind in the line reach the obstacle and back up slightly, as if considering. Then a few of them adjust direction a little and stream past their fallen colleague, apparently unmoved by her plight.

'Well, thanks,' I say bitterly, looking away. 'You don't need to rub it in.'

But Luigi is shaking his head. 'Look again.'

Three ants have stopped moving and split off from the rest of the group. They are arranging themselves around the one on its back, pedalling its legs. It takes some time for them to work it out, but soon they have hoisted her back onto her feet and set her on her way.

Luigi puts a hand to the small of his back as he straightens.

'And there we have it,' he says, limping away from the bedside table.

'There we have what?'

'*Ants*,' he says meaningfully.

I wait for him to continue. He doesn't.

'Look,' I say, 'you can't just show up claiming you're going to release me and then give me some cryptic shit about ants. I don't know what you're trying to say. Obviously, I'm supposed to be the one on my back. Or is that you? And the ones who help… what's that got to do with anything? Seriously, I'm starting to wonder whether you're just here to torment me.' I break off as he begins to climb down the stairs with his awkward gait: one, *two,* one, *two,* one, *two*… 'Where the hell are you going now?'

'Kitchen. Peckish. I'm sorry to have to point it out,' he continues gently, 'but you don't ever check on my needs. Understandable, maybe, but you have become, shall we say, rather self-absorbed. And it's hungry work, believe it or not.'

'Sorry,' I mutter. 'Help yourself. But, please, *tell me what you mean about the ants*.'

I catch his knowing smile before his face disappears from view.

'It will emerge,' he says, 'all will emerge.'

The uneven step continues for a while, and then it stops. I know he has gone again.

I bury my face in my hands for a few seconds and let out a growl of frustration so loud that Whitney seems to hear, because her tail splashes out the surface of the water for a second. I go back to watching the army of ants in silence. Where are they even going? I wonder. And then I think of the humming walls and imagine that under the paintwork and the plasterboard are whole battalions of them, moving and working together, so that the walls really are alive, filled with a rippling sea of black.

Someone is knocking on the door. Max never forgets his keys, but perhaps leaving on a flat note this morning distracted him. Maybe he can't concentrate until we've cleared the air. Maybe he'll worry that his knife will slip in surgery, or he'll sew up the wrong tubes. Entire instruments have been left in the body after operations. Apparently, that's really a thing, not just a plot device on medical shows.

I do a mental scan of my body as I walk down the stairs. It's a warm afternoon and I feel weak, but not entirely poisoned – about one-third scarecrow. The garden looks very green and I have a sudden longing for the outside world, the feel of my body moving through the air, the sense that I am going somewhere, even if it's without a purpose. Perhaps I can ask Max to put a chair out there and soak in the sun for a while, although the last time I tried that I walked back in, elated – *I'm well! I just needed some fresh air!* – and then crashed heavily in The Pit for several hours.

By the time I reach the front door, I'm feeling giddy at the prospect of spending time with him. Thank God he's come back. That's the thing about Max: he's a grown-up. He really shows up when it matters. I'm wearing one of his white work shirts with the sleeves rolled up because I've run out of anything clean that can reasonably be called nightwear. I undo a button, ruffle out my bed-hair and throw open the door with only semi-ironic sickbed allure.

'Would the doctor like to see me now?'

The man in the hallway keeps a straight face.

He's holding a very tall bunch of blue flowers, and has a newspaper tucked under one arm.

'Sorry to disappoint,' says Jesse.

'From Mrs R,' he says, handing me the bunch. 'Who says sorry about the mess, but she'd do it again if it meant getting to meet you. She was very insistent on delphiniums.'

I mutter some thanks, grateful the flowers are tall enough to hide the unbuttoned shirt, hoping they don't highlight the colour I can feel in my cheeks.

'And this is from me,' Jesse says, pulling out the paper. 'I couldn't resist doing a couple of clues while I was waiting for the flowers to be wrapped. Three down is particularly good.' He seems as relaxed as I am wrongfooted, leaning one shoulder against the door frame. 'Mind if I have a peek?' he says, peering over my shoulder. 'Always been curious to see what it's like down here. The same as our ground floor, right? Just higher ceilings and… oh, that's cool, with the bed up there.'

I step back to let him in. He's taller than I remembered and looks a bit different from last night, although he hasn't shaved. Clearer-eyed, perhaps; brighter. He's wearing jeans again and a khaki green sweatshirt that matches his eyes. In the natural light, I realise his skin is several shades darker than mine. I imagine how pallid I look. What was it he called me: the sick girl from the basement? I have a sudden urge to show him pictures of how I was before all of this. Climbing a volcano in Morocco. Galloping bare-back down a beach. Roaring around Italy on my Vespa.

'So there's a window up there?' he's asking. 'Cool view. Must be like that Disney movie, *Lady and the Tramp*, where you only see humans from the knee down.'

I nod, wondering where the cat's put my tongue. It's the first time I've had someone over since I gave up on visitors. But Jesse doesn't seem bothered about my sickness. He doesn't ask me how I'm feeling, let alone speak to me like I'm on the wrong side of a border, stranded in another kingdom. It is both a relief and strangely daunting. Have I completely lost my social skills after rotting away for months in bed with only a goldfish and a ghost for company?

'So that's where the damage is,' he is saying. 'Mrs R says to let us know when it's all dried out and she can send in the decorators. Okay if I take a look up there too?' And before I get the chance to answer, he's walking up the stairs to our bedroom.

Too late, I remember the photo of the Rothwells. My stomach does a little flip. Last night I slipped it in the drawer of my bedside table. But this morning I took it out again to study, and I can't actively remember putting it back. Fifty-fifty, it's sitting by the bed, on full display.

I drop the flowers and paper on the table and try to follow him up the stairs quickly, but my legs start wobbling, so I have to slow down. Jesse has stopped talking now; there's a worrying silence. I picture him holding up the photo, thinking about what he's going to tell Mrs Rothwell. *That neighbour of ours who you took a shine to? She's actually a kleptomaniac.* And how would I defend that? *So there's this Renaissance nobleman who says he can release me. He keeps telling me I need to break some rules.*

But when I get upstairs the drawer is closed. There's no sign of the photo. Jesse is standing, hands on hips, looking up at the ceiling.

'Pretty cool how you can see where all the pipes are,' he says. 'Like the house's innards. Sometimes I feel like this building is alive. Do you know what I mean?'

I know exactly what he means, but I find myself shrugging like a teenager. It's disconcerting, us both being up here. A virtual stranger in my place of isolation. This small square that has held all the loneliness and pain of the last five months. He's walking around, examining things, picking up Max's clay figurines, studying the painting of the couple on London Bridge.

'So this must be Whitney Houston,' says Jesse, taking a step towards the bowl. 'I should have brought a gift for her too.' He peers in. 'Quite the looker, I see.'

I'm wondering how to usher him back downstairs when his gaze falls on the computer sitting at the end of my bed.

'Are you able to work yet? Or is it just for old movies?'

Neither, I tell him, something about screens depletes me very quickly. Although a couple of hours before he came in, I had been on a Zoom with Sebastian Rose. It comes out like a boast, a name-drop, and I want to take it back immediately. But he takes it in his stride. 'Ah, yes. I hear you produce that celebrity podcast.'

I feel slighted and flattered all at once. That *celebrity* podcast. But also, *That* celebrity podcast. As if it's a thing.

'That's right.'

I ask him if he's listened to any.

'I have, yes.'

I wait for him to expand. He doesn't.

He sits down on the yellow chair. I stare at him in annoyance. What kind of response is that? *I have, yes.*

Not: I have, it's great. Or even: I have, not totally my thing, but really well produced. Well done you. But: I have, yes.

'Actually, it's not a celebrity podcast,' I say, a touch coolly. 'It's more of an exploration of how big events in your life can shed light on...' I hesitate for a beat too long.

'Celebrities?' he fills in, laughing at me.

'On high-profile people's authentic selves.'

Authentic self? Now I'm quoting from the dire press release, which I've been begging to rewrite for years.

Jesse looks amused. 'My mistake then. Which episode did you most enjoy working on?'

I cast around for a non-celebrity guest. The only one with a shred of gravitas that comes to mind is the Shadow Home Secretary. But that was a particularly ghastly interview, a bald attempt to offset some bad press after making his girlfriend take his points on her driving licence.

Jesse is watching me intently. He leans forward. 'Can I be candid?'

I cross my arms again. 'Depends.'

'I've no doubt at all you're a very talented producer—'

'But you think it's all a bunch of bullshit,' I break in. 'Yes. I know the critique of the show. That actually it's the worst kind of falsehood, this manufactured display of vulnerability celebrities now trade in, which seems so authentic and relatable but doesn't come close to a private truth.' I think of Sebastian Rose again, his face up close to the lens. 'Sure, there are some elements of *positioning*, but—'

Jesse shakes his head.

'Not that. Look, I'm probably the last person who's got anything useful to say. After the last few months, I'd have given my right arm to get down half an hour's material, authentic or not. So please aim off anything I say, maybe I'm riddled with envy.'

He hesitates.

'Well?' I say, slightly mollified.

'It's not so much the interviews I have a problem with.' He leans forward. 'It's you.'

'*Me?*' I sit down on the end of my bed in shock.

He nods. 'Peddling the idea that everyone is a product of their stories. Don't you worry that's a dangerous line to sell? The footballer who knocks around his wife, but can't help being that way because of his authoritarian dad. The actor who smashes up hotel rooms because he was locked up in boarding school aged seven. Don't you think you have more of a choice about whether your past becomes your story?' He leans back, hooking an arm around the chair. 'Also, well,' he smiles, cupping his chin in his hand, 'I know you're the producer, but I guess I hoped somehow… I'd hear your voice too.'

For a few moments I am left speechless. I haven't been able to find words for how I've been feeling about my job for months. I thought I was just getting irritated with some entitled guests, but Jesse is right, I'm at fault too. I'm the one packaging up pain, making it all too neat. Which was precisely what Gracie had been hinting when I shut her down that day in Brighton. I have a sudden urge to let it all spill out. The way the past keeps pushing itself into my sickroom, leaving me with questions and doubts. This creeping sense that I'm out of sync with myself as well as my body, that I'm fighting to avoid parts of my life I don't want to face: my job, my relationship, and how I left things with Gracie. That I worry they add up to something I can't quite see but is circulating in my system, becoming part of my chemistry, and that is somehow getting tangled up with the illness too.

But this last thought sets off such a spiral of anxiety that I sit up abruptly, trying to summon the anger that I know will shut everything else out.

Jesse has stood up. He walks closer to my bedside table and stoops to pick up something from the floor. It takes me a moment to realise what it is. The envelope that I'd forgotten to bring up for Mrs Rothwell.

'Wow,' he says. 'We've been looking for this.' He turns it over, looks at the torn end and then shakes it over the bed. Some medication slips out, a box of pills, the seal obviously broken.

I feel my ears burn.

'I didn't open that,' I say quickly.

I look suddenly at the yellow chair, as if Luigi will be there laughing at me.

'Really, I didn't.'

Jesse is looking at them. 'It doesn't matter,' he says. 'What matters is, I think you can help her.'

I have a thing about hands. Not just men's hands, the pleasure that they can give (though there is that). But because hands, when studied properly, hold many clues. Often more than the face, which can mislead or tell a lie.

We've gone back downstairs to the kitchen and Jesse is telling me how he first met the Rothwells. An advert on the pinboard of his music school; he'd moved in as a live-in-tutor to their daughter, Maya. At seventeen she was already a loose cannon, breaking hearts and writing off cars. While Jesse is talking, one hand is opening and closing in a gentle curl, while the other is running along the rough grain of the tabletop. I keep having to remind myself to drag my eyes away from his hands to his face. Eventually I give up and, resting my cheek in my palm, I gaze down at the table as if I am letting my eyes drift off somewhere neutral while listening.

Because Jesse's hands are wonderful to behold. Very broad and strong, but perfectly in proportion, each knuckle a smooth knot, the wide, square fingernails cut very short. As he strokes the wood, the tendons and veins on the back of one hand ripple and then disappear all the way up his sinewy lower arm. In the curl of the other, I catch a glimpse of callused finger pads. Both are in constant motion.

Maya and Mrs Rothwell had a difficult relationship, and her grief was especially complicated, Jesse is saying. Not that it can be anything but complicated, losing your only child at twenty-four…

I look up. *Wait, the daughter died?*

This was about five years ago, Jesse continues. The hands pause for a moment, fingers interlacing. Mrs Rothwell coped by throwing herself into her work. Became pretty famous on the concert circuit. Then she got ill. Really ill. Her lungs, he is saying… something about her mood slumping… her will to live… Jesse's voice is low and sincere. I know I should be listening but…

I look back down at his hands and find myself drifting again. This time into a different life altogether. Somewhere rural and remote. Rugged rather than picturesque. Big boulders and waterfalls, a wooden cabin. Jesse on a chair hunched over his guitar, scribbling down chords on a pad; I am writing at a desk looking out at the view. A screenplay rather than a podcast script, perhaps the biopic of a forgotten female adventurer. When was it that I'd chosen the life of the scientist over the artist? All my boyfriends until Max had been the Danny Cousins model, unstructured and artistic. What was it that drew me towards the more conventional life now? Was it fear?

Is that what Gracie meant when she said I'd be choosing the wrong story, for all the wrong reasons? What was it that Mrs Rothwell said? *That's what I want. A man who can hear the music...*

'Vita?' Jesse is staring at me. 'Look, I don't want to put you on the spot, but what do you think? Can you help?'

Shit. Completely lost track. The dead daughter. Something about Mrs Rothwell's being ill... Her state of mind. Those hands, loosely entwined now, waiting.

'Explain again why you think I can help?' I say carefully. 'I mean, me specifically.'

He nods. 'Last night she lit up for you. I saw the old her, the performer who loves people, who loves life. Before she lost Maya and Col. And this morning she won't get out of bed again. Being pretty slow about these things, it took a while for me to register it, but you're around the age Maya would be now. You even look a bit like her. I know you're sick and I know it's a lot to take on—'

'Most of the day I can't get out of bed.'

'Right. But I heard you talking to Mrs R about how the illness comes and goes. So I wondered if... just the odd visit,' he says, and his palms press briefly into a steeple, fingers touching his chin, before he stands up. 'You don't have to answer now, just think about it.'

When he gets to the door, he pauses for a moment. 'That picture you have, of the couple looking stuck in the city. Do you find it hard to look at sometimes?'

For a moment I think he's spotted it after all, the photo of the Rothwells. My heart crashes against my ribs. Then I realise what he's talking about. Upstairs on the wall. Max's painting. The lovers on the bridge, captured still while the crowd is a faceless swirl of paint around them.

'How do you mean, "hard to look at"?'

He swings the door lightly between both hands. 'Maybe it's just me. I've started to see them everywhere, the walls of the city. I need to get out, to exist in open spaces, look out at the sea—' He breaks off abruptly, smacking his forehead. 'Sorry, that's tactless of me. Given how stuck you must be feeling.'

I nod. 'Wildly tactless.'

He hovers, uncertain.

'You should be ashamed of yourself,' I add.

He breaks into a smile of relief.

'So you'll consider it, then, coming upstairs?'

12

Donkey Ride

After Jesse's gone, I go back to bed and lie gazing at the painting on the wall. I can feel the aches in my legs, the pricking pains around the base of my scalp. Any minute now the sledgehammer headache will fall. If I keep on staring at the two people on the bridge, maybe it will stop me from going under.

But Jesse is right, the painting *is* hard to look at. It's not just the corny neatness of the idea; there's something else that irks me. The walls of the city, Jesse said. The picture made him feel hemmed in. Me too, I realise. Though I'm not quite sure why.

'Claustrophobic. It makes you feel claustrophobic about Max.'

My eyes ping open.

Luigi is sitting in his usual place, his arms stretched overhead, fingers interlocked. He flips them over and cracks his knuckles.

‘Everything you worry about what he wants from love,’ he says. ‘That he sees it as a refuge, rather than an adventure. A recharging station before heading back out to where the real action is. That’s why you’re feeling hemmed in. Because he’s trying to fix it in a frame. He wants love to *stay still*.’

I frown and sit up straight. The pain has gone, or at least it seems to have. I have a strange moment where I picture myself from afar, still resting back pale-faced on my pillow with my eyes closed, eyelids twitching as I dream my way out of The Pit.

‘That’s Gracie’s view, not mine,’ I say, then add suspiciously, ‘I don’t see how you could know… wait, you haven’t been speaking to her, have you?’

‘Of course not,’ he sighs. ‘I don’t spend much time socialising where I come from.’

We both look at the painting again. Now it’s impossible not to see a couple who are stuck in the city. No wonder it made Jesse want to go and look out at the sea. I breathe in, recycling the stale air in my bedroom. My mind drifts and I can hear the crunch of small stones under my trainers, the sting of salt in the air.

Gracie stoops to pick up a flat pebble from the stony Brighton beach. Her newly dyed hair is luminous pink in the afternoon sun.

‘Veets?’

'Yup.'

She gives me a sidelong look, fingers the edge of the pebble and in one movement whirls around and sends it skimming across the waves. It bounces once, twice, then disappears.

'Do you ever think of her when you look at the sea?'

I start walking again.

'No, I don't. That was a lie,' I say, shortly.

'The Big Lie,' says Grace. 'That we all played along with. Wimps that we are.'

I keep my eyes fixed on the frills of foaming water lapping close to our feet.

'It's been a big day. Can we talk about something other than the past?'

'No past. No Max,' she says dryly. 'What is there left to talk about?'

'A bit of not-talking would be wonderful,'

'Fine.'

We pass a stack of unused deckchairs, round the back of a cafe and cross onto a new stretch of the beach. This part is almost empty. Perhaps there's a change in the direction of the wind, but the suck and drag of the waves over the pebbles sounds louder here. Halfway down I can see a sign reading 'Donkey Rides', a couple of children bouncing around in the saddle as they're led down the beach.

'Are we still being cowards?' Gracie picks up, as if we haven't just walked for ten minutes to nothing but the sound of the waves. 'Carrying around all these secrets after all these years. I mean, why don't we blow those doors open now? Sit down with all of them, talk about what really happened?'

It would sound oblique to anyone else, but it's the closest we've ever got to discussing that day in the basement. I feel my skin prickle, cold water pouring down my spine.

I make a quick calculation.

'Let's get a couple of donkeys.'

She shadows her eyes to gaze down the beach then looks back at me with a grin. 'You reckon?'

'Your last day in Brighton. It'll lend it a biblical feeling.'

The donkey lady has nicotine cracks on her fingernails and a long wispy ponytail. A few minutes later, we're both crying with laughter as we bump along the pebbly beach, our feet practically dragging against the ground as two pairs of giant ears twitch in front of us.

'Can't believe this is happening,' says Gracie, breathlessly, as we manage to pull them back into a walk and rock along happily beside each other, the donkeys' little hooves splashing on the edge of the water. 'The only biblical thing about this will be the size of my arse later.'

Her donkey takes off again so that she is forced to bounce in the saddle double-speed, but mine doesn't. Instead it plants its hooves in the pebbles and refuses to budge. I flap my legs and jiggle my reins; no dice. It's just not going anywhere. I get off and pull it, it doesn't move.

Gracie has, by now, reached the end of the shingle and is trotting back. She finds me, dismounted, and having taken the reins over the donkey's head, pulling and pleading with it just to move one step further. It stays stock still, apparently bored. Then, for no reason at all, my donkey starts ambling back to its owner.

We're still giggling when we get back to the stand and pay the lady who tells us, closing the zip on her bum bag with a smile, to come back again, the donkeys love the exercise.

Maybe it's the elation of the ride and all the laughing, or maybe it's because I have to leave soon and feel that surge of love towards Gracie I always get when I stop worrying about her for a moment, but I find myself saying: 'What you said about being wimps. You shouldn't see it like that. We did what we had to do to survive.'

But even as I say it, I look away. Only half of me believes it and the words feel brittle and second-hand. Faye's Big Lie all over again. 'Your mother went to sea.' God knows why she came up with that as a euphemism for our mother's sudden death when we were young. Perhaps because we'd gone on a sailing holiday the summer before she died. But it must have suited Faye's romantic sense of herself. That our mother had abandoned her family and sailed off into a life of independence, rather than the brute reality: that Faye had moved in a few months after our mother had died from a brain haemorrhage, married our father and then cleared out all traces of his ex-wife. All clothes, all jewellery, all photos. Even the toys our mother had given us, like the fabric doll with the wide flat face and long auburn hair, just like hers and Gracie's. Burned them in a firepit in the garden and then whitewashed our mother's existence, perhaps convincing herself, and our father, that this was what was best for us too. That the past should be left behind entirely. So that we grew up with the lie about what had happened to our mother, but worse than that, a wall of fire around the subject. A fierce heat, which meant we didn't have to be told to step back; not, on any account, to ask questions about her; to keep our heads down if the subject was brought up. 'How old were you when you lost your dear mama?' a kindly acquaintance once asked. 'Their mother went to sea,' Faye cut in briskly, with a vinegary look, and that was that. Another year without her being mentioned in the house. Until we were so well trained in the omertà that soon we began to say it, too. *Our mother went to sea.*

I look up. The wind is blowing pink hair across Gracie's eyes. She is trying to tuck a lock behind one ear. 'I remember drawing a family tree at school,' she says. 'I was so scared, I put Faye's name on it instead of Mum's. Even though I knew no one would see it.'

'Not your fault.'

We've turned around and started to walk back now. A purple cloud has moved over the sun. My hands are cold.

I rub my palms together before thrusting them in my pockets. 'Let's enjoy the sound of the sea, shall we?'

Gracie shoots me a glance. 'It's amazing to me that you work on a podcast called *Confessions.*'

'Still talking.'

'Sorry.'

But the smile is back in the air between us. Uneasy because of the argument that morning, but there. We're passing the donkey stand again, but they must have gone home for the day. Looking the other way, across the dunes, I can see the woman with the wispy ponytail loading the donkeys into a trailer. One seems to be resisting, and I can just make out, from the donkey's stance and the movement of the woman's arm, that she is thrashing it to try and force it up the ramp.

Gracie doesn't seem to have noticed and is still looking out to sea. Instinctively I move to her other side, to block her view of the dunes.

It's something I've wondered about over the years. Whether it's her I'm protecting or me.

13

Another Version

I'm lying on the sofa scrolling through Instagram, on the hunt for #dannycousins and then, after multiple dead ends, for 'Jesse + musician', when I hear the sound of the loo flushing. For an awful moment I think Max has been in the apartment all the time I've been noodling the whereabouts of my ex-boyfriend (and, come to think of it, the howabout my upstairs neighbour). I close all my apps and sit up just in time to see Luigi limping out of the bathroom, straightening his doublet.

'You might want to give that a minute,' he says, slamming the door with a grimace. 'I always forget I shouldn't overdo it with the muscadines.'

'I didn't know you were here.'

He squints at me. 'You're looking guilty, Vita.'

'No. Why do you say that?'

He gives me another suspicious look and then limps off towards the kitchen. The sound of a cupboard opening, the rustling of a bag. Eventually he reappears, holding a bowl and sitting down at the other end of the sofa, breathing hard.

'Do you know that women are far more likely to run out on their partners than men?' he says, plunging his hand into the bowl.

I dart him a quick look, but he's staring into the distance with what's become a familiar expression. He's thinking about Lucina again.

I remember my shock years ago when I first read the Epilogue to 'Giulietta', a rant against the fickleness of women.

Whither art thou now fled, sweet piety and faith in woman? What living instance could we boast of that truth, proved unto death, shown by Juliet to her Romeo? How many are there, who, in these times, instead of falling by the side of their departed lovers, would have turned their thoughts only to obtaining others? Unfortunate are the lovers of this age, who can never flatter themselves, either by long devoted service, or by yielding up their very lives, that their ladies will consent to die with them.

It was the bitterness, after such high romance, that had surprised me.

'*Bitterness?*' Luigi says, as if he can read my thoughts. 'Oh, no, Vita, you have me very wrong, that was just for effect. I didn't blame Lucina for marrying someone else. Not at all. There was intense pressure on her to make a good match. And being a woman, she didn't have much say in the matter.' He reaches into the bowl for another handful. 'What *are* these exactly?'

'Twiglets.'

He wrinkles his nose, reaches for another handful. '*Christ.* Only the English could make these,' he mutters through a full mouth. 'Can't work out whether I love them or hate them. But where was I?'

'You weren't angry?'

'No, no. I was in despair. I was *broken*. But it wasn't about her marrying someone else. It was what happened in the few moments we'd had together after I'd been injured. After the horror of the battle, the terrible journey in that bumpy carriage back to Montorso, the stink of infection in the wound, the doctors shaking their heads, grim-faced, saying I'd be lucky if I walked again. All I had been holding onto, every second, every breath, was seeing her, holding her...'

'But then?'

Luigi shakes his head. 'Before she even sat down, the moment she looked at me, my twisted body with my useless leg stuck out in front of me, I saw it in her face.' He pauses. 'The *distaste*.'

'Oh, God,' I say, flinching. Because I know just how he felt. I'd not found a word for it until then, that look on

Max's face when he arrives back from work and steps up into the mezzanine to find the blind still drawn and me, slumped and puffy-faced in the same t-shirt, with a half-eaten bowl of cereal balancing on the mattress beside me, staring at Whitney Houston, lost in my circular thoughts. A look that he wipes clean quickly but not fast enough for me not to spot it, to understand in that split second how it mingles with his doubt and makes him feel so bored and trapped that it becomes a kind of repulsion. *The distaste.*

And then my own distaste – worse, dislike. For the days when I succumb to the apathy. When I can't face all the things I know I should do – the supplements, and the breathing cycles, and drinking litres of water, and the anti-histamines, the meditation, the visualisations and the goddamn positive thinking – and instead lie there under my duvet of self-pity, scrolling through my phone, which makes me dizzy and the aches come on quicker, when I can't even bring myself to look up at Whitney Houston, because I am already sliding and I forget the depression is an inevitable symptom. I feel like the author of my own Pit.

'I'm sorry,' I say again. 'Really, I understand.'

But Luigi barely hears me.

'What I realised, in that instant, was that Lucina only wanted *a particular version of me.* The handsome, dashing captain of arms who could gallop her across the hills and make love to her in forest glades.'

I gaze back up at the ceiling as he talks. For some reason I find myself thinking of Jesse's steady gaze, his ease with not knowing, his patience. Was I just imagining that, dreaming it up, seeing that particular thread in him that I'd found so sexy in Danny? Danny, who'd been fine with things that made him wait, like traffic and queues and sickness, who had never been at war with time. Who, when I sprained my ankle (lost key; silly shoes; crumbling garden wall), had faked sickness himself so that we both sat around drinking wine, playing cards and talking shit in bed, watching bodice-ripping soaps on mute and inventing panting dialogue to overlay it. Who enjoyed the mischief in me, like Gracie did. Who perhaps, if I hadn't dumped him, would have made sure—

'Oh, *damn.*'

I look up in time to see a spasm cross Luigi's face and he blanches. The bowl of Twiglets slips to the floor with a crash.

I sit up in alarm. 'Luigi! Are you okay?'

He pulls himself to his feet. 'Forgive me…' The colour is returning to his face, but he still looks haunted. 'Those blessed muscadines.' And he hobbles, much faster than I've ever seen him shift, back to the bathroom.

I pick up my phone. No emails. Just one message, from Jesse.

Thank you x

*

Later that day I dream of Danny Cousins. It's an airport scene that never happened because when he took the job in Sante Fe, a couple of weeks after we got back from Verona, I told him that I didn't do long-distance and he should leave as a single man – and that started with no crying at the Departure gate.

In the dream, though, I follow him to the airport to surprise him. Somehow, I've hitched a lift with a faceless man in leathers on a motorbike so as to get to Heathrow before him. But when I arrive, I realise I don't know which airline he is on, or which gate to go to, and when I ask, all the airport staff frown and say it would be a breach of privacy rights to tell me. So I say I am his wife, Vita Cousins, and some bad health news has just come through and I must tell him before he gets on the plane. And meanwhile I hare from one gate to the next, desperate to tell him that I love him and that I have my passport in my pocket and am ready to go, too. When eventually I spot him, he's just on the other side of the barrier, standing in line for security with a pretty brunette. They're laughing at something and he's carrying an extra bag over his shoulder, which looks like it belongs to someone else.

When I wake up it hits me. Danny was never going to get back to my email because I wasn't that laidback, independent girlfriend who didn't do long-distance, *but hey, no hard feelings*, wished him well on his way. I was the baggage, the thing he didn't want to cart around anymore and certainly doesn't want to think about now. All these years I'd told myself I dumped him, when actually he'd left me. I'd just been too proud, stubborn, inflated and insecure to let myself see it.

14
Lying

I am sitting at the piano, enjoying the sensation of my fingers resting on the cool, silky keys. With a few stumbles, I can just about play the Scott Joplin rag I learned when I was in my early teens. Mrs Rothwell is sitting next to me in the wingback chair. A large black-and-white headshot of Col sits on top of the piano, chin cupped in one hand, heavy-lidded gaze fixing on whoever is playing.

'I'm bloody glad he's not alive to hear you,' says Mrs Rothwell and starts laughing again.

I've come upstairs on the pretext of wanting to mess around on the piano. But looking at her, wiping her eyes behind plumes of vape smoke, I'm quite sure that Jesse must be mistaken. What had he said about her having bad lungs, losing her will to live? This is a woman spilling over with life, not running out of it.

'I told you, I need lessons.'

'You don't need lessons, my love. You need handcuffs.'

'So come on, you play for me.'

She shakes her head. She's been refusing all morning. 'I much prefer listening to you butcher classics. Play Für Elise again.'

'This is abuse,' I complain. But I do the opening trill with my right hand, and then fumble around for where to start with my left, which sets her off again.

'Just one piece,' I say, turning towards her. 'There's that very beautiful one I've heard you play a lot.' I hum the opening bars of the music I'd overhead while standing in the corridor.

She stops laughing. 'Ah, that's Lizst,' she says. '*Liebesträume.* Which means "Love's Dream". But for me, it's all about the heartbreak.'

So Luigi had been right. *She is very sad, is she not?… A profound sadness in her tonality.* I look back at the photo of Col.

'I'm sorry.'

'Don't be. That was Jesse playing.'

I blink in surprise. 'Jesse?'

She nods. 'A piece he learned to play for his wife.'

'*Wife?*'

She raises her eyebrows. 'He was briefly married; it didn't end well. That was why he moved in with me, after Col died. We were two broken birds.' And then, as if it is the most natural segue in the world, 'How are you and

Max getting along? Him being a doctor and not being able to fix you.'

Quite unexpectedly, I find tears spring to my eyes. I brush them away, wondering why I cry so easily around her.

She looks at me steadily, takes another pull on the vape.

'Mostly he's patient,' I say. 'But sometimes I think he suspects it's all in my head. Like some kind of Jane Austen character.' I attempt a smile. 'An attack of the vapours.'

I close the piano lid. It's the first time I've expressed this fear out loud; first time I've really allowed myself to think it.

More silence from Mrs Rothwell. I try to focus on the fact that I've come up to help her, not the other way round. But now that the words are out there, I want her validation. I want her to feel outrage on my behalf. Against the limits of the medical establishment, its proof-led myopia, its deep unconscious bias against women and neurosis.

But Mrs Rothwell is nodding. 'I wonder about this a lot. How much of sickness is linked to the mind.'

She smiles as I scowl and turn away.

'Don't jump to conclusions, Vita. Keep an open mind. That's what you're asking others to do. Everyone talks about mental health these days, but I think they are missing the point too. The brain is a lump of meat and nerves just like the rest of us. It's not mind over matter, it's mind *is* matter. Until doctors stop trying to chop the head off from the body, whether it's a sickness like mine, or a sickness like yours, they'll never fully understand.' She takes another pull on her vape. 'Tell me, have you never felt it before in your life? That your body logs all the old wounds?'

I open my mouth to protest. But even as the words rise to my lips, I feel my mind splitting off. Max in the hospital, telling his doctor friend: 'She has a history.' And all at once I'm back there. Thirteen years ago, in a room that is the colour of weak tea, a photograph on the wall of a boat stranded on the sand, surely not the best choice. A tall, bearded doctor at the end of my bed, pink lips couched in wiry dark hair, reeling off a checklist from a clipboard. Have I any difficulty sleeping; night terrors; voices in my head; suicide ideation, do I cry more than usual? I answer 'yes' and 'no'; play with the ridges of the purple terrycloth quilt, which is changed every other week, unless we vomit from the medication in which case it will be swept away immediately by a purse-lipped nurse. The family therapy meeting where Faye and Gracie are in the same room for the first time since she left home. Gracie stinking of booze, and me thinking: *She should be in here, not me.* I was the one who got off easy. I'd been packed off to summer camps when the going got tough. Gracie's eyes, glassy, cut off. The therapist asking, in front of Faye, if we were afraid of our stepmother. The toxic silence in the room. And Magnus, Faye's son, chewing gum and not bothering to hide his smirk. The group therapy session when I first hear the term 'survivor's guilt'. The microwaved jacket potatoes for lunch whose brown skins have lifted from their dirty innards. The girl in the room next to me, connected to an IV for anorexia, who will be carted off to hospital soon where she will die, her parents pleading with her to have a mouthful of a banana. The family friend who came to visit me when her nephew was sick with cancer. Who told me to get over myself because some people have real problems. The steel nit comb left by my bedside, its sharp teeth that I focus on for minutes or hours or days, wondering how much damage you could inflict if you pressed it into skin hard enough.

The guilt. The guilt. The guilt.

I look up at Mrs Rothwell. The lamp casts an uneven shadow. I have a ridiculous urge to tell her everything. Instead, I clear my throat, hear myself saying, 'I thought I'd left all that behind.'

She nods, as if I've said much more. Then asks me whether perhaps Max is not a doubter at all, whether he's just a good enough doctor to understand that the mind and body and nervous system are talking to each other all the time. And that this doesn't make it less real, it just makes it deeper.

I stare at her, caught by this possibility. Not sure whether it is true. Suddenly not sure of anything at all.

'You remind me of my daughter,' says Mrs Rothwell, leaning over her vape. She's unscrewing the lid, squeezing drops of sweet-smelling liquid inside. 'Not quite sure why.'

I don't know what takes hold of me then. Perhaps it's gratitude, or sympathy. Perhaps it is thinking about that time in the hospital. A door I normally keep closed in my head, swinging open.

'Maya, wasn't it?' I ask slowly. She jerks up her chin, her face blank, confused as to how I would know this.

It's then that I see the fork in the road.

I can tell her Jesse told me her daughter's name.

Or I can lie.

'It's the weirdest coincidence,' I say. 'I knew her.'

To lie convincingly – I read this in one of those free magazines you get on the Underground – steal as much as you can from real-life events. Maintain eye contact for seventy-five percent of the time. Less is shifty. More is creepy. Never touch your face, especially your mouth. Try not to swallow. Swallowing is a dead giveaway. As is smiling too much. Visualise the lie, so you feel you are describing it, not making it up. Use as much detail as possible.

So that's what I do.

I tell her about how we first met, in the basement of the Crowne Plaza, off Hanger Lane junction. One of those grimly functional hotels where you have to hole up for the morning with a hundred other pissed-off people, drinking watery coffee and eating dry biscuits. *Speed Awareness Course*, they call it. In other words, a conference room full of dangerous drivers.

Mrs Rothwell, whose face has drained of colour at the mention of my knowing Maya, laughs. 'Sounds like my girl…'

She and I were at the same table, I tell Mrs Rothwell. I noticed that she was attractive, my age, mixed-race, nothing more than that. On her left, a plump minicab driver wearing pointy slippers who fell asleep straight after the first coffee break. Which wouldn't have been funny, especially as he smelled of alcohol, but in the middle of being shown slides about zebra crossings, he gave out a little piggy snort. Maya and I exchanged a glance. And that was that. The next two and a half hours became an exquisite agony of trying to hold it together. Each time a new grunt or whistle emanated from the sleeping form, I had to dig my nails into my palms. At one point, trying to look elsewhere as the laughter bubbled up, I saw her shoulders shaking. I had to leave the room, then. We both ended up in the Ladies, cackling so hard we had to switch on the hand-dryer to cover the noise.

I slip my hands under my bum on the piano stool while I pile on the details for Mrs Rothwell. Tremors are sweeping through me. It hadn't occurred to me, though now it seems obvious: lying affects the central nervous system.

But there's no stopping now. Mrs Rothwell is glowing with each mention of her daughter. 'I do hope you're not over-taxing yourself,' she says, as I try to hide my shakes. 'I can't tell you how much this means to me. It's like... it's like being in the room with her again.' Her voice chokes a little. 'God, I've missed that.'

I've just begun to describe our journey back, via a pub in Shepherds Bush, which I tell her was Maya's idea ('Of course it was,' breaks in Mrs Rothwell, with a pained smile), when I catch a movement out of the side of my eye. My whole body prickles cold, then hot.

'You'll have to excuse me,' I say, standing up from the stool. 'I think I need to lie down now.'

Jesse steps into the room then. He's wearing a navy blue t-shirt and jeans, a net of satsumas dangling from one hand. I've no idea how long he's been there.

'I'll walk you downstairs.'

Mrs Rothwell agrees with this idea, insisting I accept the help, but as we leave, she calls me back. Her voice sharp, like something unpleasant has occurred to her. 'Vita. A question.'

Here it comes, I think. She's seen through me all along: *'So you're a liar as well as a thief?'*

She leans back so that her eyes are in shadow.

'You will tell me more next time?'

Jesse and I don't talk until we're at my front door. I'm genuinely short of breath, and he seems lost for words.

He leans against the wall, his hands in his pockets. The neckline of his t-shirt is lopsided. 'I guess I should thank you,' he says.

'By which you mean: I took things too far.'

'Well, yes.' He gives me a slow, deep smile, and I feel something turn over inside me. 'Totally nuts. Morally reprehensible. But also, a stroke of genius. I haven't seen her that happy for years. So, whatever it takes. Also…' He hesitates, and I can't quite tell in the awful lighting but perhaps a little more colour comes into his cheeks. 'Something shifted for me that night you came up. Maybe it was a sense you could help. That it all felt a bit less suffocating. Like, I don't know, a change of key. I think that's why I've been writing better since. Not brilliantly, but not so shitty either. So whatever you did for her, thank you. Not that it's relevant, but it helped me too.'

I'm so surprised by this that I stammer out some kind of moronic banality. *Oh, that's great*, or *So pleased to hear that*. Or maybe both.

Before he leaves, he puts his hand on my arm. It's just a brief moment, maybe it means nothing. But the feeling stays, long after he's gone.

15

B Sharp

Grief does something to a face. There's a heaviness to the eyes, a dullness to the skin. A bunching of muscles, not just along the jaw, but between the neck and the shoulders, as if the body is braced to fend off the next wave of pain. I see it in Mrs Rothwell the moment she opens the door. Old grief, revisited. For a moment it's like I am staring through a looking glass. I have a flash of sitting in a garden behind a crematorium in North London, the freshly upturned soil around a sapling, the feeling of a mildewed bench under my thighs.

Then Mrs Rothwell blinks, smiles, and it vanishes.

'You made it to the summit again!' Her face is bright with relief. 'I was worried that all the activity knocked you out.'

I think of the thirty-six hours since Jesse left, tangled up in sweaty sheets and hallucinations, trying to focus on

Whitney Houston through the waves of pain and fear. I shake my head.

'Liar!' she says kindly. 'Well, come in. I'll ask Jesse to fix us some coffees when he gets back from the market. I have a new machine. Serves up wonderfully pretentious things like ginger shot lattes. Of course, I've no idea how to use it. Careful you don't catch your foot there, that damn carpet flaps.'

Her hair is slicked back from the bath I heard running out just a little earlier. Without the framing of her bob-cut, her face looks more creased and fragile. Her throaty voice, so beguiling and decadent the first time we met, lands differently now.

I run through the choices I discussed with Luigi as we walked up the stairs.

Option A: Tell her I made a mistake about Maya, claim brain fog, disordered mind, etc.

Option B: Claim descent into further sickness and don't visit again.

Option C: Let's see how it goes.

'Tell me if it's not a good time?' I say to Mrs Rothwell.

'On the contrary.' She cocks her head. 'Unless you'd rather come back when Jesse's here?'

Oh, *haha,* no. 'Didn't mean that,' I say.

She looks at her watch. 'He'll be back any minute.'

'No, no,' I say. Flustered now. 'Just didn't want to intrude if you're enjoying a bit of time on your own...'

‘Hell, no.’ I follow her into the living room. She tells me, her breath staccato from walking, that *me time* – as those ghastly lifestyle magazines like to call it these days – is the last thing she needs. ‘My head gets too crowded when I’m alone. Jesse is the same. We distract each other as much as possible. It keeps the ghosts away.’

I have a flash of Luigi, sitting on my yellow chair waiting for me, arranging his cape over one shoulder to best effect, checking his pouting reflection in the window. Funny how, for me, it’s the other way round, I want to tell her: I have this vain, bombastic ghost who distracts me from things I’d rather not be thinking about.

‘I imagine you find that, too,’ says Mrs Rothwell, sucking in a breath before dropping heavily into her armchair. ‘You must be alone for hours in that flat, with Max so busy in the hospital.’

Ah, yes, busy Max. Who everyone thinks of as permanently bent under bright lights, deep in some life-saving operation, rather than hiding from the boredom of my illness, gossiping with Izabella about hospital politics.

I murmur something non-committal, caught by the idea of Jesse trying not to think about his ex-wife. I’m still struck with wonder as to her existence. Who was she? Perhaps a singer. Preternaturally talented. Not some hack grubbing away on a ghastly celebrity podcast. Layla, she’d be called. No, Ava. I think of Max’s assertion that I spin jealous fantasies around women with exotic names.

Perhaps Ava had died. An accident in the Alps… A falling cable car…

I look up to see Mrs Rothwell, her eyes laughing at me. 'Well, aren't you going to ask me more about him?'

I do my best to look blank.

'Jesse.' She stretches over to the top of the piano and picks up her vape. 'Or are you, *haha*, not curious? He's certainly getting keen on you. Last night I was telling him what a great guy Max is, how kind he'd been the week Col died, and Jesse said, "Bet you a tenner she's too good for him."'

I blame it on my mother, a redhead, that I blush easily. My whole body flushes crimson and my scalp prickles when I'm on the backfoot.

I open my mouth to tell her a half-truth, that since I met Max the people I find myself most curious about are other women, but then blow it by backtracking.

'Jesse told me he moved in as Maya's tutor,' I say. 'He called it a refuge.'

She nods. 'His parents were very uptight people. Bible Belt. Fixed views. They didn't like his passion for music, thought it was an indulgence. Then in his teens, when he was experimenting a bit, they caught him with a boyfriend. Turfed him out, no questions asked. He wound up couch-surfing in London. That's where Col and I came in. I guess we were the family he would have chosen. But he's never quite found his home since.'

A boyfriend. I keep my voice casual. Make it not quite a question. 'Then he got married.'

Mrs Rothwell looks pained. 'That was recently. Lara. A disastrous year and a half with a woman who called herself a "free spirit". Took him months to work out that it was a synonym for "covert narcissist". Longer still to walk out.'

'And that's when he moved back in here? To… help out?'

It's the closest I've got to suggesting Mrs Rothwell is not in perfect health. She cuts her eyes away, takes another drag on her vape. 'The timing suited us both. But I worry now that love and duty have got tangled up. He needs a bit of a push—' She breaks off suddenly. 'Ah. Speak of the devil.'

A scraping of keys in a lock, the slamming of the front door.

'To be continued,' murmurs Mrs Rothwell, just as Jesse walks into the room wearing a honey-coloured cord jacket with one collar up, carrying a small box in one hand and a couple of vinyl records under his arm. His skin is flushed; he seems to be wrapped in the outside air. I find myself checking whether he wears a wedding ring. Those hands… he doesn't.

'Oh, *hello!*' He looks obviously delighted by the sight of us together. 'Did I interrupt something?'

'No,' I say.

'Yes,' corrects Mrs Rothwell. Then her eyes drop to the small box he's holding. She curses and checks her watch. 'We've missed the start!'

'Only a few minutes. I'll grab coffee. You take these,' he says, handing me the box, which is surprisingly light.

'Is there something I can help with?' I ask, puzzled, as Mrs Rothwell bends over the side of the chair and starts patting the floor underneath.

'Damn thing always goes walkabout when you most want it,' she says, reappearing with a remote and pointing it like a gun at the flatscreen TV. 'Open that, will you, dear?' she adds, gesturing with her chin at the box as she scrolls channels. 'You're in for a treat.'

By the time Jesse comes back carrying three coffees, I realise I'm witnessing a ritual. The box contains two Portuguese scorched custard pastries ('You can share mine,' says Jesse. 'Yes, share his,' agrees Mrs Rothwell), which they both eat while sipping their coffee, eyes trained on the TV.

'Look at this new contestant,' says Jesse. 'He's going to be brilliant.'

'I don't think so,' says Mrs Rothwell, her bottom lip covered with crumbs. 'The ones that look that nerdy are often a disappointment. Brilliant on the specialised subject, no doubt. But he'll come a cropper on the general knowledge round, just you wait.'

I haven't seen *B Sharp* before. It's the kind of thing I'd flick past immediately if I came across it during a rare instance of watching live TV. (Who even does that anymore?) A daily quiz show on the subject of music.

'Good pun for the title, though,' I suggest.

They both look at me disapprovingly.

'That's the worst bit,' says Mrs Rothwell.

'"B sharp" is actually a "C",' agrees Jesse. 'No musician would *ever* call it that.'

Within moments it becomes apparent that the two of them watch it religiously.

'This girl hasn't been knocked out for seventeen days running,' says Mrs Rothwell, waving her half-eaten pastry. 'Don't be fooled by the braces. She may look fifteen but she's a card-carrying genius.'

'And we think she's developed a severe crush on Richard,' adds Jesse, gesturing at the host who is cheesily handsome with a long face like a potato and obviously dyed, wavy black hair, 'which is really putting Maggie's nose right out of joint.'

'Maggie has never married,' says Mrs Rothwell, gesturing at the glamorous co-host. 'But her last boyfriend looked just like Richard. Except more unattractive.'

'Even more unattractive,' agrees Jesse.

They both nod at the TV and take a bite of pastry in unison. They look so similar, in fact, that for a moment, despite the difference in colouring and features, I'd swear they were related. I think of what Mrs Rothwell said about how Jesse would have chosen Col and her as his family. Can you ever really choose family? I wonder. As we reach the climax of the episode, a timed 'Beat the Intro' round, Mrs Rothwell and Jesse are both on their feet shouting out answers at the screen, alternately hurling abuse and pleading with the contestants. Can you really replace those who've never shown up for you, or who you've lost?

Over the next two weeks, I come every day. Luigi advises me to write a journal of my symptoms, something I've previously been loath to do for doctors. But he's right; it helps establish a pattern. The rhythm means I remember to take the off-label drug which finally arrived in a little brown bottle from Glasgow. The doctor gave it, with suspect precision, a one in eight chance of working, but it's certainly doing something: trippy dreams and, I like to think, fewer aches. I discover that if I rest through the morning, do my breathing exercises, stay away from too much trawling on Chronic Fatigue forums, social media or anything else that spikes my adrenalin, I am usually clear for a good couple of hours in the afternoon to come up, eat a custard tart while watching *B Sharp* (Jesse, since day two, has always bought three), then stay until I run out of steam or one of Mrs Rothwell's students pitches up for a lesson. I pay for it later, of course. The Pit always collects. But it feels like progress to be able to bank on even just a few hours of symptom-free sanity at a regular point in the day. For the first time in months, I feel like I'm getting better. *I won't need you soon*, I tell Whitney Houston, who glides past again, unconvinced.

For the first couple of afternoons I arrive with ready-made anecdotes about Maya, but although she is referenced occasionally, Mrs Rothwell doesn't ask me to talk about her at length. Once, when Jesse is out of the room, she asks me if Maya ever mentioned her. This is a question I've prepared for. I give a little sigh.

'Only once that I can remember. She said the two of you had a "difficult love affair".'

'Did she really?' Brightness gathers in her eyes.

I nod.

'That's good,' she says, looking away for a beat too long. 'That's very good to hear.'

Looking at the slant of her shoulders, I feel a wash of horror at the enormity of my intervention. Why had I felt it was okay to rewrite such a delicate part of her history? And yet her relief is so palpable, like she's put down some terrible weight she's been lugging around for years, that it feels like it must be the right thing to do, to give a sick old lady some reprieve from her constant agony.

Most of the time she is so lively and irreverent that I can't believe what Jesse has told me. For a woman who is in her seventies, ill and grieving, she is very robust. It doesn't seem like the behaviour of a depressed person who is giving up on life.

Which is what starts me thinking. I begin to wonder – and these are fantasies I allow myself at night when I wake to find Max's side of the bed empty again, or when one day I'm late for a *B Sharp* and Jesse texts me asking where I am: *Oi. You coming?* – whether the whole situation has been exaggerated by Jesse to bring me more regularly into their lives. To lend him some support with Mrs Rothwell, of course. But also maybe, just maybe, because he feels it too: this strange warping of space–time between us. As if every hour we have spent together is being cashed in within a different time zone, skipping over several hundred datelines, adding up to more than it is. So that it feels, somehow, like we met each other long before we did. That there's a version of us out there already, existing in the future, waiting for us to catch up.

'Jesse is the kind of man I see you with in the end,' says Luigi, who has taken up residence in the yellow armchair again.

There's a bowl of pistachios beside him that he must have unearthed from the downstairs cupboard. He scoops out a few and starts cracking them out of their shells. 'When I go through all the nearly-but-not-quite boyfriends in your life, he feels like he's something different. He may look like Danny, but the one he *really* reminds me of is Massimo.'

Massimo. I sit up in surprise. I hadn't thought about Massimo in years.

'To set the record straight,' I say, plumping my pillow and stacking it behind me, 'nothing ever happened between me and Massimo.'

Luigi throws back his head with a snort. 'Do me a favour,' he scoffs. 'You had a more meaningful relationship with Massimo than plenty of people you had sex with.'

I open my mouth, then close it again. To be fair, this is true.

Massimo and I had met one evening in Verona, not long after I arrived in town. I'd been wandering around Piazza Erbe as the light faded, waiting for Danny who'd been 'caught up' with work again. I was scattering the remains of a disappointing cheese *panino* for some pigeons when a small black-and-tan sausage dog crashed into my ankles, nearly knocking me over.

'Pronto, no! *Pronto…*' A man with dark curly hair and a crumpled pink shirt came rushing up. 'Sorry for my dog. She thinks she is a pigeon.'

By the time Danny texted, two hours later, Massimo and I had exchanged life stories as we strolled around the piazza ('The problem with Pronto, silly dog, she only pees when we're on the move'), and agreed to take her for a passeggiata the following day. Which we then did, every day for the following two weeks, long lunches or an evening walk down the banks of the Adige with Pronto trotting at our heels, none of which I breathed a word about to Danny.

Luigi smiles as he cracks another nut, collecting the shells in one hand. 'So nothing came of it with Massimo, I know. But he was a way of swapping out Danny.' He pauses, tosses the pistachio up into the air and catches it in his mouth, 'Just as Danny was a way of swapping out Jamie. You eclipse every exit with an entrance. So, here is my question about Jesse: is he a real beginning? Or just a way of dodging another goodbye?'

I wince. Gracie used to say much the same: 'Your love life is like a relay race.'

'Jamie *Green*?' I push back. 'Oh, no, him you're wrong about. We split up before I even went to Italy.'

But the words die on my lips. Luigi is smiling knowingly.

And all at once I'm back there, on that hot, painful, dizzy day. Wrapped in Jamie Green's warm arms beneath the coloured mural wall in the Porta Nuova train station. A goodbye hug that had somehow turned into a hungry kiss. His neck wet with my tears as I swore to him that he was the love of my life; something that in that moment I believed, utterly.

Jamie Green, with his sandy freckled face and kind eyes, who I'd met at a fancy dress party in our last year at college, wearing a bee-keeper's outfit. Who I'd persuaded to ditch his degree in biochemistry and follow his dreams of being a film-maker, and who had moved with me to London, where we lived in Kings Cross above a Sichuanese restaurant – the food was so packed with chillies that when the windows were open our eyes watered. And who had flown out to Verona to ask if we were still together, because I'd dodged telling him it was over, and strung him along, letting him think I was there on my own, rather than following Danny, Jamie remaining firm in his belief that I would come back to him. And who I had kissed in the train station again, rather than release him, because I couldn't stand an ending, couldn't stand the silence it left.

Then, walking back into town, the rising sense of self-disgust. A feeling like I couldn't breathe under the blazing sun. It was then that I'd passed the church with its giant open door where a hushed coolness drew me inside. Fractured light streaming in through the stained windows, spilling colour down the aisle. At the back, a pale effigy of a bleeding Christ, neck twisted to one side. And the side chapel, with its oil paintings, which I would have walked straight past except my eye snagged on the descriptions in Perspex frames, a few lines translated into English. 'The original author of Romeo and Juliet'. And that look that came back from Luigi. *What took you so long…*

I look up and see him watching me. I glance over at Max's side of the bed. For the last few days I've been asleep in the morning when he's left for the hospital. Is that who I am? A coward who runs away from endings?

Luigi sighs and sweeps some pistachio debris from his lap. '*Amore mia,* do not travel too far up your own arsehole. That is Max's job. All I am saying is that I like Jesse, and I like the fact that you are feeling better.'

And he's right. I do feel better.

During this time I rarely see Max, who stays longer hours than ever at the hospital, preparing his pitch about the clinic to potential investors. After the Izabella call, on the few occasions we do cross over, I don't tell him that I've been upstairs again. A fact that Luigi, legs crossed and one eyebrow raised, finds 'deeply interesting'.

Things take on a pleasing, secretive rhythm.

Apart from two days, when I fall back into The Pit and can't leave my bed, the poisonous aches and weakness dragging me down into the vortex, I begin to look forward to the afternoon as soon as I wake up. When the three of us are together I don't feel self-conscious at all. It doesn't just feel like a holiday from my illness, but from myself. Neither of them asks me how I'm feeling, or about my job or my relationship, the coordinates with which other people pin me down. And yet it doesn't feel like a lack of curiosity or disinterest in my life. Rather, some kind of unspoken pact we've made to keep ourselves in the present.

Once, I witness them having a real argument.

B Sharp was already on the TV when I walked in, but neither of them was watching. Jesse looked grim-faced; Mrs Rothwell had that rebellious expression that I'd seen on the first evening when they'd been fighting over the whisky.

'Hullo,' he says, barely looking up as I walk in.

'We're having a domestic,' says Mrs Rothwell, flashing me a look.

'Oh, right,' I say awkwardly. 'Want me to come back later?'

There's a mutinous silence. Jesse stands up and begins to pace the room.

'Came back from the shops and she's sacked the lot of them,' he says in a tight voice.

I glance from one to the other. 'You'll have to explain.'

'Her students,' says Jesse, wheeling round and glaring at us both. 'The children she teaches. Whose lives she lights up, and vice versa. I come back from my walk, and she's called around every single one of their parents, without even discussing it, and told them she can't teach anymore. As from today.' He clicks his fingers. 'Just like *that.*'

I sink down onto the sofa. It's hard to imagine a world in which I don't hear scales trickling through the ceiling every day. But is it really so bad? Maybe you get fed up with teaching Grade One by the time you're seventy (maybe you never weren't fed up of teaching Grade One).

Perhaps she's just got to the point when she wants to play for pleasure?

'Is it getting… tiring?' I ask Mrs Rothwell carefully.

She shrugs and cuts her eyes. 'I thought I might give the piano away, actually.'

Jesse starts pacing again. I've never seen him like this. 'Does it mean *anything* to you that I live here?'

'You know it does,' says Mrs Rothwell quietly.

'And now all this bullshit about bequeathing me the flat. You know I want to get out of this city.'

'Fine. So sell it.'

'But I can't fucking sell it, can I?' says Jesse, his voice raised. 'Col lives here. In this piano. Between these walls. On that chair. And besides, when did you get so fucking defeatist? Why do you get to decide when to pack up your life? It's morbid –' he takes a deep breath, as if preparing himself '– and selfish.'

'Just being practical, my dear,' says Mrs Rothwell, calmly, and I remember what she said about love and duty getting tangled up. About Jesse needing a little push.

On two occasions, I glimpse a different side of her. Once, after the show has ended and we're debating whether Maggie has pumped up her lips, I notice she has gone unusually quiet. There is a waxiness to her skin, a listlessness that I saw on the first day she opened the door. I'm about to ask after her health when she stands up and, without looking at either of us, announces in a flat voice that she can't stand the racket we're making, that she wants to lie down – and no, she doesn't need any help getting to her room. I half-stand up, but Jesse shakes his head at me abruptly, and it's as clear as if he's spoken. *Leave her alone. She means what she says.*

Another time when I arrive at the door, it's not on the latch as usual. As I raise my hand to knock I hear her crying, mixed with the low mumble of Jesse's voice, and the strumming of a guitar. I recognise the tune he's playing, some love song I feel she's mentioned in reference to Col, but I can't remember the title.

I turn away and go slowly back downstairs.

Then one day I come up to visit and Jesse turns me away.

It's obvious from the moment he opens the door that something is wrong. His tan skin looks sallow, his normally clear eyes bloodshot.

'Not today,' he says.

I feel a drop in my stomach like a lift has just plummeted several storeys.

'How is she?'

He shakes his head fractionally. Bad night. She'd coughed up blood, then been unable to sleep for the pain. This morning a migraine.

Coughed up blood. My stomach drops another level.

'What can I do to help?'

It's a stupid question. I know this. People want little tasks when you're sick. They want to feel useful and active in your recovery. What they can't do is what you most need; to bear with the stasis, the lack of progression, the stuckness.

'Will you let me know how she is?' I say, turning away to walk back down the stairs.

I'm stopped by a hand on my arm. Turning back, I feel my heart speed up. Jesse is only a few inches away from me, closer than we've ever been. The air between us begins to hum.

'Thank you,' he says. 'I don't know how much it's cost, you coming up every day—'

I begin to shake my head but he stops me, touching a finger to my lips.

'You've been amazing for her. I've seen the light in her these last two weeks. Not just bursts of fireworks, like she can do for others. But a steady light. And something else too. A calmness, or as close as I've seen, since Maya, to peace.'

I stare at him helplessly. Wondering at the sudden, exquisite familiarity of his face, trying to remember how it felt that first night we met, with him standing in the doorway. Then his gaze seems to drop to my lips – or does it? – and for a long, surreal moment I'm terrified that I will lose control, that I will step forward and kiss him.

And then I do.

*

The feeling of another man's mouth on my own. The warmth of his lips, the shock of a different taste. Max always smells of coffee layered over toothpaste. The taste of Jesse's mouth is strangely raw; a sharp saltiness to it that makes me think of sweat and smoke and earth. His tongue meets mine, forcefully. I feel the graze of his teeth and with it an explosion of fear and exhilaration, like I've surprised myself with a much too high cliff-jump into the sea. Except I'm not falling; he's solid and warm in front of me. Until, with a sudden movement, he's not.

The humiliation doesn't come immediately. I stagger slightly, trying to regain my balance, too surprised to register what's happening.

Jesse has taken a step back.

'I'm sorry…' he says, breathing hard. 'I'm not your way out. I'm not sure what I am, but I'm not that.'

Before I've had time to utter a word the door closes.

And I'm left with shame.

16

Basement

The swell of poison catches up with me halfway down the stairs. I know it's going to be a bad one. Most of the time my body gives me warning signals, a red light blinking on a machine, but this time the safety alerts are swiftly bypassed, like a great, grey wave crashing through flimsy flood barriers.

I don't know how I make it to our front door, or lift my shaking hand to fit in the key, or make it up the steps to bed. I do know at some point I'm crawling on all fours and crying, using the treads of the stairs to pull me up, like a soldier who has been injured on the battlefield. But I'm in the darkness on the way down to The Pit, and I know I have to get there first. Another wave is coming towards me, a breaking wall of pain and horror. The only way I can survive it is to take one more lungful of sanity and dive deeper still, under the riptide. Back there, to the one place I don't want to be.

*

I'm walking down the stairs again. This time there is a metal handrail on the wall. When I get down there, I know it will be a different basement. Eleven-year-old Gracie will be waiting for me. She came to find me in my bedroom, but as soon as she started to speak, I knew we weren't safe. Upstairs in Faye's house, all the walls have ears.

Gracie and I call the basement flat 'the womb' because of its dusky pink walls. It has its own external entrance, behind a line of symmetrical pot plants, but you can also get to it by walking down the steep stripped-wood stair behind the kitchen where there is a door with a cream ceramic doorknob and a silver key that always sits in the lock below it. The flat is almost always busy with lodgers: a single teacher; a young married couple; for six golden months it became a refuge for us when a young trainee nurse from Romania with long black hair asked us down to have tea and custard creams after school and sang to us. She left, though, when Faye found out. Occasionally when we are between tenants, it is empty.

When I get there, the door is already unlocked. The cupboards have all been taped up after the end-of-tenancy clean, and everything is covered with dust sheets, misshapen lumps of oatmeal, including the sofa where Gracie is sitting. She's not crying but her eyes have that glassy, broken look I remember from the log ride a few months earlier. It doesn't occur to me that it can be anything other than Faye's fault.

*

That clamp on the back of my head now, a pair of forceps. Squeezing my brain like it is trying to juice it. No nutrients are left. Just a fossil that, with a bit more pressure, will explode into a dust cloud. Stabbing pains, needles of fire around the backs of the eyes and the temples. The only thing to do is breathe through it. In through the nose, out through the nose. Don't use your mouth. Nasal breathing is better for activating the parasympathetic system. Remember this too will pass. Water, I need water. I can see half a glassful on my bedside table. A day or two stale. It will have dust settled on it and be the blood-warm of room temperature, not the icy cold which feels like it can help chase out the toxic sludge. And if you can't do that, if you can't will your hand to raise and close around the fat stem of the glass, then look over at Whitney Houston circling her bowl. Except now even that doesn't seem possible: changing the direction of my eyes against the iron curtain of torpor. The resistance to do anything apart from sink into it, although you know you shouldn't, like an Arctic explorer succumbing to the deep sleep of the freezing that will mean certain death.

And I'm back down in The Pit again, and that other basement, too, with the low pink ceilings and the wooden slatted shutters. 'His door was open,' Gracie tells me, small hands pleating the edge of the dust sheet like she is trying to gather up her senses. He called her over as she walked past it to go down the stairs. Magnus. Seventeen years old, mainly away at boarding school, or tennis camp, or weekends with friends, but home now for the summer holiday.

He told her to come in and close the door. Patted the side of the bed for her to sit next to him. He was wearing boxer shorts, pale green and white checks.

'Go on,' I say, when she stops.

Gracie starts to cry as she tells me. How he put his hand around hers to show her how he wanted it. *Gently*, he told her. *Now faster.*

Gracie is gripping the dust sheets and crying so hard she can hardly speak. Then she chokes and starts to breathe too quickly. I tell her to calm down, that it's all okay. That she's with me now. Like my heart is not crashing against my ribs. Like I'm not as revolted as I am, with him – but also with her. It's okay, I repeat, putting my arm around her shoulders. And while I wait for her to breathe and tell me more, I look at the framed botanical prints on the walls, try to ignore all the strange, dark thoughts going through my head. Like whether it meant Magnus thought she was prettier. Whether that was why he hadn't picked me.

The floorboards creak overhead. Gracie and I simultaneously tense, as if we're listening out for prison guards. It's easier to tell Faye's footsteps than anyone else's in the house. They are light and quick.

What else happened? I ask. And she tells me, nothing. Nothing after the white stuff came. 'That's it,' Magnus said, reaching for a towel, 'game over.'

I look at Gracie, scratching her wrists and all over her lower arms like she's suddenly sprung a rash, when something else occurs to me. Was this the first time it happened? Gracie starts crying again, and says no, the second. Then she looks at me and her eyes are pink and her face is streaked with tears and her nose hanging with snot. 'What am I going to do, Vee?'

I look at the folds in the dusky pink curtains, the slight shine on the curve of the material and the darkness between. When the dust sheets aren't on, they match the sofa we're sitting on, as well as the walls and the cushions. Something tells me that this is an Important Moment in My Life. Although that doesn't seem right, because the big thing that happened was up there in Magnus's room. Not down here in the darkened room with the dust sheets.

'I'm going to talk to Faye,' I say firmly, although my stomach drops. 'What happened was…' I pause, searching for a word that is not too damning '… horrid, but I'll make sure it never happens again.' I have a sudden stroke of inspiration. 'What we're going to do is walk back upstairs and leave what happened down here in this room. It will stay behind, we can lock it away. You never have to think of it again.'

'That's it?' asks Gracie, wiping her nose with the top of her wrist, looking both bewildered and relieved.

'That's it,' I confirm, suddenly feeling confident of this course of action. 'But you have to promise, Gracie,' I look at her sternly, 'you'll never come down here again.'

'I won't,' she says and hugs me very hard. 'I swear I won't.' Then she thanks me like I have saved her life.

Before we leave the womb, I tell her to wash her hands. For some reason I wash mine too. Then I lock the door behind us.

It's lifting now. I'm rising up from The Pit and back into my present basement. Luigi is sitting waiting for me on the yellow armchair. He has his leg crossed and is examining the cuticles on his left hand. The relief of seeing him is so enormous that I don't know whether I want to laugh or cry.

'Thank god you're here! I've never been so happy to see anyone in my whole life.'

Luigi continues to study his nails.

'Luigi?' I say.

No answer. I glance over at Whitney Houston. She is not circling the bowl as usual, but hovering over the padlocked treasure chest, staring at me accusingly.

'Luigi!'

He sighs and recrosses his legs the other way round, as if he is bored of waiting.

I say his name half a dozen times before it sinks in that he can't hear me. As soon as I realise this, he starts to fade, becoming more transparent, so that I can begin to see bits of the room through his torso, and then his head, until finally, he disappears.

And it's then, only then, the horror lands. That I never shut it away in the basement that day. That we've been locked in there all this time. Gracie most of all, but me too, in different ways. In those five weeks when they committed me to hospital, and now perhaps, lurking in my nervous system, dredged up by the sickness, and grief.

17

Otherwise

Dusk or dawn? If I had to guess, dusk. The ceiling of the mezzanine flashes on and off blue, which I know means something. I can't find the file in my memory, though. My senses seem to have detached from my brain. There's nowhere to process input. Doors slamming and raised voices somewhere outside. Turning my head, I see the back end of an ambulance through the window onto the street. The bottom half of people in green and high-vis overalls, a loud rattle as they pull out a ramp. Moments later the sound of doors opening and shutting upstairs and then a thunder of footsteps. Low, urgent voices coming through my ceiling.

I arrive back on the surface and sit up, gasping for air.

Mrs Rothwell.

It doesn't take me long, by current standards, to get out of bed, walk down the mezzanine steps, then up to the ground floor. Maybe nine minutes. But I know I'm too late well before I reach the top of the stairs. The front door has slammed, leaving a loud silence.

Mrs Rothwell's door is closed too. My arms feel like wet spaghetti as I try to bang on it, calling Jesse's name. The same stupid, selfish thought going round and round. I have to explain. The stories about Maya, I was trying to help. No, no, I just have to tell her I'm sorry.

I lay my ear to the door. No sound at all coming from within the flat. He must have gone with her. My knees buckle and I slide down to the floor. Too late, too fucking late again.

I'm lying on the sofa when Max returns home. I've been staring at the photo of Mr and Mrs Rothwell, which I've taken out of the drawer and propped on the coffee table next to me. I don't turn around when he comes in.

He leans over the back of the sofa and drops a kiss on the top of my head. 'Who's in the picture?'

'The Rothwells. Took it from her flat.'

'Took it?'

'Yes, stole it. After the flood.'

Silence. I picture him raising an eyebrow. Perturbed, but allowing for a certain amount of eccentricity from the sick girl, not really wanting to know why.

'But you'll give it back?' he says casually.

'Not anytime soon.'

I tell him about the ambulance through the window, the stretcher and the noises overhead.

'Oh, dear. Sorry to hear that.' Max starts to take off his jumper, wincing as he pulls it over the shoulder he dislocated when I jumped down from the mezzanine into his arms after I proposed. It never quite healed right. Then he sits down, picking my feet up and placing them on his lap. 'How was your day otherwise?'

Otherwise is everything you need to know about Max. A whole life story could have been carried out his front door on that stretcher, a whole love story. A lie, a deceit, a betrayal, and Max would find an 'otherwise'. It's something he's always been praised for: compartmentalising. I can see the upside when you're cutting someone open. The problem is when that becomes a way of living, when you can't sit with any sort of confusion without wanting to sort it all away. The messy; the mad. Because things that get tucked away start to rot, a series of corpses in the basement, subtly infecting not just you, but everyone above.

'How are your patients?'

For a moment or two Max looks wary. I can see him trying to calculate my mood.

'You don't actually want to talk about them,' he says.

'I do.'

He squeezes my feet and gives me a small smile.

'They're fine, Vita. Why don't you tell me how you are?'

That way he uses my name, as if I'm the child and he's the adult.

But the smile, that's the worst thing. The slightest upturn of the lips, a picture of calm knowingness. A smile that says: I know exactly what's happening here. You're looking for a fight because you're feeling neglected. Except he's wrong. It's easier for him to think I'm needy; some weak, needy woman who wants more of him, than to wonder about what really goes through my head in these absent lonely days.

'I don't care about them more than you, Vita.'

'I never said you did.'

He shakes his head, as if he knows me better than I know myself. I wish he did. I wish he knew the darkness. I think of Jesse and feel an odd, empty guilt.

'It's just there's a difference.' He gives my feet another squeeze, a little too hard this time. 'I care about you, but I need to take care of them. Because they're really sick.'

Really sick? As in, actually sick? As in, I'm not? The vague feeling of guilt falls away.

'I get it,' I say, pulling my feet away. 'They're really sick.'

A hunted look darts across Max's face.

'Oh, come on, Vita. Of course I didn't mean that. I just meant, they're very ill.' He flinches. 'Which you are too. Look, it wasn't a comparison.' He sighs, rubs his eyes. 'Honey, don't do this. I've had a long day… Just… why don't you tell me what's going on?'

I think of the scrape of Jesse's skin against mine, Gracie pleating the dust sheets, Luigi vanishing, myself in a sobbing heap in front of Mrs Rothwell's door.

'Do you really want to know?'

I catch Max's eyes flicking to the photo of the Rothwells. I can almost hear him thinking, *I don't need this shit. I spend all day saving lives, then I come home to this.*

'Of course I do. Wait, let me put on the kettle first, I'll fix some tea. You can take a breath and figure out what you're really feeling.'

'I know what I'm feeling.'

'Yes, you do. But I can see that you're angry,' he says carefully. 'Maybe if we take a moment—'

Maybe if we take a moment the madness will die down? Or maybe I'll start feeling too weak to express it. Or maybe I'll worry that you can't handle it, so I'll back down? You're right, maybe that will happen. So let's not take a moment.

I lean forward and look him in the eye. 'I don't think that I can bear this anymore, what's happening to me.'

He smiles sympathetically. 'I hear you, my love.'

'No, you don't. You're not listening. I have visitors. Most days it's a jilted Renaissance ghost who wrote *Romeo and Juliet*. He has views on my love life, as you can imagine…' I hold up my hand as Max tries to interrupt. 'He's not the only guest. I have fantasies about past boyfriends – did I ever tell you that Danny Cousins dumped me, not the other way around? And apparently I've spent my life using relationships to numb myself against my upbringing. That was a blow. And, oh, recently I've been fantasising about the guy upstairs.'

Max's face is drawn, scrubbed of emotion. I imagine it's how he looks when he walks into the operating theatre. I take a deep breath. Too late to stop now. 'Of course, I've been telling myself the same lie too. That there's nothing wrong with me. Aside from all the shit that's going on with my body, I mean. Because that's what we do. That's how we've learned not to frighten men off. But the truth is, it just makes us angry. And more than a little mad. Because we're squashing down the bits of us we know you can't handle. Whether that's in the attic, or the basement, or the fucking bedroom. And somewhere along the line that means we start to forget who we are, too.'

'You want to sleep with the guy upstairs?'

I look him in the eye. 'Yes.'

Max stands up, his body rigid. The dents around his nostrils have gone white.

'That's just sick. Why would you tell me that?'

'You're right,' I say, beginning to laugh. 'I should have kept it to myself. But I'm starting to learn how much better I feel when I'm being honest. At the moment, the most real relationship I have is with a ghost and a goldfish. But I'm afraid if I tell you about them, you'll just think I am nuts after all. That the sickness isn't real. That it has all come from my head.'

Max's eyes flicker.

'*Tell me,* Max. Does it ever occur to you that medicine may still be in the black-and-white era waiting for Technicolor to come along? Can't you see it in more shades now, given the case study you've been living with for the last few months? Let me save you some time: the sickness is real. There's a *real* bug in the system, a virus with a fierce grip burrowing into the organs and the nervous system, wreaking havoc with physical weaknesses and trigger-happy immune systems. But here's the thing… the mind, the biggest bundle of nerves of all, plays a part in that too. And medicine, your medicine, can't begin to untangle it, let alone measure or heal it. So it dismisses it and it diminishes it. It tries to make it all our fault.'

Max is leaning against the wall, with his face in his hands. The rims of his ears have gone very red, and the skin around his neck is blotchy. I feel a part of me detach from myself, stepping out of my body and observing the scene with a kind of thrilled fascination. Am I about to watch the highly esteemed second-youngest consultant colorectal surgeon in the country completely lose his shit?

'Really?' says Max. 'I think there's nothing wrong with you? *Really?* Don't demonise me as some binary fuckwit who doesn't understand what you're going through.' His eyes drop, he can't look at me. 'You know what? I think it's the other way round. All that doubt you accuse me of… It's your doubt. About me. *You're* the one with the trust issues. *You're* the one who can't believe in *me*.'

'Give me a break,' I snap. But his words run down my spine like cold water. I feel found out, somehow.

He leans in, he's not stopping now. 'Here's what I think, Vita. I think everything is wrong with you. And that vicious, mysterious bug preys on it all – the grief and the scars and the memories and the half-truths. And I love you, for and despite of, all those things. Which is something you don't seem able to understand. It kills me not being able to help. I hide in work because I can't bear being so useless, not knowing enough. Medicine is partial, and it understands very little. It fails people.' His voice cracks a little. '*I* fail people.'

'Oh, spare me the self-pity,' I mutter, feeling a new surge of rage because not-knowing is exactly what excites Max. All those gaps in medicine that people like me fall through are projects to him, frontiers to be crossed, Nobel prizes to be won. 'Well, you better get used to failing,' I say, my voice hard. 'You all failed Gracie. You let her die.'

'Gracie?' He shakes his head in disbelief. '*Now* you want to talk about Gracie? You won't mention her! Not a word, you shut me out every time. I've tried, God knows I've tried. But you keep locking me out. Jesus, Vita. Do you know what that feels like? Seeing you in pain. Struggling, stuck. It's like you're trying to stop time, because then…' the slightest pause '… she won't have died.'

I open my mouth, casting around for the sharpest, meanest words I can hurl at him, but nothing comes out. For a few minutes we sit in silence, exhausted by each other.

'You're right,' I say slowly. 'I am being visited by some broken ghosts. One of whom is my sister.'

As I say this, I feel a great tearing inside of me. And into this breach rushes all the pain I was never able to feel as I sat on the bench in that North London crematorium, staring at the spindly little sapling in a mound of earth that was supposed to mark where Gracie was. Except I knew she couldn't be there because we hadn't spoken since I'd left her in the train station two weeks before. And I couldn't feel any sadness, either, because I knew this couldn't be it, not when she was only getting started. Because it hadn't just been that day; for that whole year when I'd visited her in Brighton, I could see she was really changing – she was happier than I'd ever seen her and for the first time she was excited about where she was going. Because my number was the last one she dialled on her phone before she got into the shower the morning after I left and she had her final fit.

So instead I just sat on that bench and let myself go numb. Another door locking behind me.

I breathe through the pain and turn to face Max. 'It suited me to think that Gracie was the broken one. That it was her on the run, not me. Perhaps I had to get ill before I could slow down enough to see it.'

Max is staring at me, like he's never met me before. Perhaps he never has. He's doing sums in his head, I can sense it. For a moment I feel him trying, I feel him grappling to fill the new space between us.

'I'm sorry,' I say. 'It isn't your fault. I think I just had to get angry to be able to tell you.'

He nods slowly and walks to the door. He's had a haircut, I realise belatedly. There's a little strip of paler skin below his hairline.

'And will it help?' he asks, without turning around. Below the bitterness, a faint note of real curiosity. 'All this shit you've dug up? You really think it will help you get better?'

I think of Luigi. *I'm here to release you.*

I don't know, I think. Perhaps I even say it.

By the time I look back, the door has already shut.

18

Departures

As soon as the door closes I feel very cold. This has always happened to me, even before I got ill. The tips of my fingers lose colour, turn white. Gracie's gloves are on the shelf, under the mirror by the door. I haven't put them on since the day I left her.

We had arrived at the train station ten minutes early.

Usually Gracie never walks me here. Neither of us is good at goodbyes. ('For obvious reasons,' says Gracie. 'Or just because it's awkward,' says me.) But today she is insisting on it, which I know means she's still feeling bad about our fight this morning.

The temperature has nosedived since we were on the beach, as it can at this time of year. It's dark outside now and the forecourt of the station is enclosed like a giant warehouse. The slats on the roof, part opaque, part glass, block the wind but retain no heat, so that the air is cold and still, like a fridge.

We buy two cups of tea, which neither of us want except for warming reasons, and sit at one of the round metal tables outside the cafe, watching the digital ripple of the Departures board. My train doesn't have a platform yet.

'Thank you for today,' says Gracie, dunking her teabag. 'I couldn't do it without you, you know that. The move. The new start.'

'Just make sure this one actually lasts,' I say, then wish I hadn't. I sound morally superior, again.

I look back up at the board. Still no platform, though now it reads: *Preparing.*

'Your lips are going blue,' says Gracie, peeling off her gloves. 'Take these. No, come on. You feel the cold more than I do.'

I hesitate, but she thrusts them at me, and so I put them on, grumbling about what's the point of gloves if they are fingerless? Fine, just for a few minutes, to warm me up a bit.

'About this morning,' says Gracie softly.

'Let's forget about it,' I say quickly. 'You know me, I already have.'

She looks down at the table and shadows move across her face, changing her features. From the precious few photos we've ever seen of our mother (passed on surreptitiously by our maternal grandmother), I know Gracie looks the most like her. The same heart-breaking symmetry to her face. When it isn't dyed, the same shade of autumn in her hair.

'Oh, look,' I say in relief. 'Platform eleven.'

We get up and walk towards the barriers.

Gracie trails behind me. 'Veets, one thing,' she says.

I pause reluctantly. Whatever it is, I'm pretty sure I don't want to know.

She faces me, a little breathless. 'What I said about Max. The way I've behaved towards him recently… none of it's fair.'

I shake my head slowly. This isn't what I was expecting. 'So why, then?'

Gracie takes a breath. 'It's me being selfish, trying to keep you for myself. Max is the first person I've seen who can really hold his own with you. Sometimes I think you're not ready to settle down, that you're just racing for safe harbour again, but I've realised I'm not able to judge that straight. The point is, there's nothing wrong with him. He's great. I'm a cow. Maybe you're not ready for him, but he really loves you, as do I… No, shut up, let me finish.' She sucks in another breath. I can see what this is costing her. 'My problem was, I wanted you all for myself. You've always fought my battles, and I was scared that you wouldn't be able to do that anymore if you were with him. But I know that's bullshit. You'll always be there for me, Veets.'

'Gracie, I—'

'Endeth speech. The peroration is over. Amen. You're going to miss your train if you don't step on it,' she adds, glancing at the clock. 'Seriously, go!'

I hug her briefly.

Then turn and run.

It's not until the train has pulled out of the station that I hear those words again, *You've always fought my battles*, and I allow myself to go there.

Remembering the dread as I climbed the narrow stairs to Faye's studio at the top of the house. Like a hand pushing back against my chest, turning my legs to lead. A thick rope is strung up in loops to make a handrail along the wall. I pull on it hard as I get closer to her door, letting it burn my palm.

It must be her sixth sense, but Faye is very nice to me from the moment I walk in. She tells me to take a seat, that she's been wanting to see me. Would I like to try one of those chocolates in the round box? Someone sent them to her. And some jasmine tea, made from real flowers. It's a special thing, she'll put on the kettle now.

It's a bright day, sunlight pouring through the skylight window. Everything is a dazzling white including the floorboards. There are only a few bits of furniture, made from either very pale stripped wood or wicker. On the walls are her paintings: white orchids against a white background, folded white napkins, a plain notebook with empty pages. A heavy smell of turps hangs in the air. It is a beautiful, disinfected, whitewashed world.

Faye is wearing an old-fashioned smock, made from some kind of heavy linen material with little diamond-shaped pleats at the chest, her pale hair twisted up. She pours boiling water into a delicate glass mug over what looks like a small, tightly packed ball of straw.

'Watch it for a moment,' she says. And we sit in silence as the jasmine bud unfurls, like cramped fingers slowly opening from a fist, and begins to show its spiky magenta heart.

'Isn't it magic?' she says, flashing me another smile.

It takes a good few minutes, with me running through the lines I've planned to say in my head, before it comes out in a rush: I have something to tell her about Magnus and Gracie. Then I dry up and look down, playing with the edges of a white cushion that I'm holding. The jasmine flower looks like it has bloomed too far now and is sinking to the bottom of the glass. My tongue has turned to stone.

Faye seems to understand.

'Why don't you forget I'm here,' she says gently, 'and tell it to that cushion?'

And so I do. I gaze into the white square until I can imagine I am not really sitting in that uncomfortable wicker chair at all. My voice feels like it is coming from somewhere faraway, as I relate, more or less verbatim, what Gracie told me. Sometimes the words stick in my throat, but then my sister's crumpled face comes to mind and I force them out.

When I've finished speaking, I realise I still cannot look up to face Faye. Because although I thought that was the hard part, I see now that all I have done is taken the pin out of the hand grenade. It's been unspoken lore in the house that we don't criticise or complain about Magnus. What will happen if this is transgressed has never been tested.

'Do you want one?' says Faye, with a smile in her voice.

I look up, confused.

She has opened the round chocolate box and is offering the first one to me. They are very dark, each one dotted with a tiny flower of crystallised sugar, rose-coloured and lavender.

The relief that I am not in trouble, that some horrible punishment is not about to come crashing down on my head, is so profound that I feel myself sag in the chair.

Boys could do silly things at his age, she is telling me. But she and I both knew, the thing about Gracie – and here she lowers her voice confidingly – is that she likes to exaggerate. A bit of a drama queen. One day she should make a very good little actress. It's one of the advantages of having lost our mother: both of us will grow up to be creative, Faye is quite sure. *Now.* Am I going to take one of these or not? They are handmade chocolates, the lavender is the best.

The padded casing crackles as I pick one out and hold it numbly between finger and thumb.

'Well?' Faye laughs as if I have done something a little infuriating but somehow charming. 'Are you going to eat it or watch it melt?'

I try to reply but the reference to the 'loss' of our mother has utterly floored me. It's like we've been playing cards, and she's whipped out the ace of a suit that I didn't even know existed. Not 'gone to sea' but 'lost'. Finally.

I put the chocolate in my mouth and although it tastes like soap, I pronounce it delicious.

'Excellent!' she laughs, jumping up. Then she tells me that she wants to show me the painting she is working on right then. A white seashell, whose glossy pale pink curved lip disappears into shadow. When I tell her it makes me think of secrets, she laughs approvingly, tells me I always was the clever one.

When I walk out the white-washed room, back down the narrow stairs, I know that what Magnus did will never be mentioned again. Gracie will be waiting for me downstairs, and I will have to lie. I will invent a story of a conversation we never had, in which I stood up to Faye: about Magnus, about our mother, about the whole crazy way she tries to change our reality. I will not tell my sister that when it came to it, I didn't push back. I was easily disarmed.

But the funny thing is, despite the burn of the rope on my hand and the taste of lavender in my mouth, I don't yet feel any sense of guilt or betrayal. I feel hope. That Faye and I can be allies.

Because she could do that, Faye, with her flashes of charm and intuition and her beautiful face. She could make you think that being loved by her was possible.

The train is hurtling through the darkness at top speed. Away from Gracie, back to London and Max.

When I look up at the mirrored glass of the window next to me, I see a woman staring back at me, crying. It's only when I raise my hand to wipe away my tears that I realise I forgot to give Gracie back her gloves.

19

Confessions

'Okay… Testing.'

'Where do I begin?'

'Just your name, in a normal speaking voice.'

'Luigi da Porto.'

'Again. Your surname only.'

'Da Porto.'

I wince, lifting an earphone off. 'Your *p*'s are popping.'

Luigi looks startled. He glances down at his breeches as if he may discover what I'm talking about.

'Your *p*'s,' I repeat. 'You're too close to the mic. Pull your head back a few centimetres… not so much… Okay. Let's try again. Use some *p*'s.'

We've turned the yellow chair so that it's directly facing the table at the end of the bed, and the microphone is set up at the other end to Whitney Houston's bowl.

Luigi holds his head still and speaks clearly into the mic.

'People from Perugia prefer pornography.'

'Perfect,' I say, grinning.

Although I've explained to him that there's no audience and it's not being filmed, Luigi's turned up with freshly washed hair, a careful side parting – which gives him a touchingly boyish air – and a freshly pressed white linen shirt with elaborate ruffles at the wrist. He looks like an actor playing a Renaissance nobleman in a high-quality Netflix drama.

We've gone through the format of the interview briefly. He will make some kind of 'confession' first, and then start bringing in different parts of his life; at least that's how it normally runs. In this case, I suggest, it might be a little different. Perhaps he can talk about how events in his life – his time with Lucina, of course, but other ideas of romance, too, perhaps the relationship between his parents – explain why he came up with this particular love story.

Luigi had nodded at this when I suggested it, but now his jaw looks very tight and there's a faraway look in his eyes, which never bodes well; a nervous guest is a dreadful interviewee. I have no idea what he might bring up, but my guess is that he'll have spent one too many centuries thinking about it.

'Remember,' I tell him as I begin recording, 'this is just for fun. So relax and start by telling me a few basic things about yourself. Think about it like you're simply talking to me. No one in real speech would say, "My name is…" They'd say…'

'Hello, I'm Luigi da Porto,' he breaks in, in a warm natural tone. 'I am forty-four years old, or five hundred and forty-odd, depending on your point of view. I was born on the tenth of August fourteen eighty-five in Vicenza. I was, or at least tried to be, your typical Renaissance man, a writer, a fighter, a country gentleman. Until I was twenty-six years old and went to battle for the last time.'

He pauses for breath and looks up at me. 'Okay so far?'

'Wonderful.' And I mean it. 'Now just explain what most of your modern audience will think of as the headline: that you're the guy who came up with the story of *Romeo and Juliet*, however many years before Shakespeare.'

Luigi leans carefully into the microphone again.

'Except I didn't,' he says.

He'd been nervous about that battle, for some reason. Perhaps being in love did that; made you feel more mortal. The stakes were higher; life held so much more meaning since he'd met Lucina four months before. But his chief fear was of dying, of not being able to see her again. The thought of being badly injured had never really occurred to him.

It was a nasty bit of luck on the day, 19 June 1511. There had been an uprising in Friuli against the Venetian Army.

He'd been on horseback when he was struck by a spear in his neck. The chainmail covering the join between his helmet and the rest of his armour must have flicked up at the wrong moment – it was a bit of a design fault, if he's honest. The next thing he knew, he was being picked up by two of his men, one at his head, one at his feet, shouting instructions to each other as they carried him off the battlefield.

They took him to the field hospital – just a handful of makeshift beds, made from sacking – on the riverbank. Although still within earshot of the battle, there was some shelter from the sun and a fresh water supply. Luigi couldn't feel the left side of his body at all. There was blood trickling down his brow and across one eye and this strange pulsing at the base of his head like his skull was trying to explode. But the young soldier in the bed next to him was in much worse shape. Luigi didn't recognise him, but he must have been around the same age, possibly a year or two younger. Also from Vicenzo, but not a nobleman, he could tell by the accent. Like Luigi, he was lying in his undergarments, but had a deep rapier wound in his side. It was obvious he was losing blood fast. Every few hours his bandages would soak through, and a boy who couldn't have been more than fourteen would dart up to him, clean the wound and apply new dressings before attending to the next soldier.

Even from where Luigi was lying, he could tell the other man was dying. And the young man knew it too.

'I don't have much time,' he said. Breathing through his teeth to manage the pain, he then asked Luigi two questions.

'Do you have a good memory? Are you able to write?'

Luigi reassured him that he could do both; that he was in fact a writer of modest… well, let's say *moderate*… success, and had published a few volumes of poetry. The young soldier looked at him in amazement and relief. Fate had laid them side by side, he told Luigi. He had something very important to relate. And although his skin was now the colour of marble and he was sweating so much his hair was wet through, he started to tell Luigi the story of his Giulietta.

I've been scribbling down some notes, but at this I look up, wide-eyed. Luigi gives me a terse nod, as if to say, *No, you didn't hear me wrong,* before cutting his eyes. He ploughs on.

Giulietta came from a rival family to his own in Vicenza, the young soldier told him. There was some petty dispute between the two houses, no one remembered the cause, but they had been in deadlock for a generation. Then one night, he was walking past her house and he heard the most beautiful voice singing from a balcony…

'It was love at first sound,' the young soldier told Luigi. Which seems impossible but it wasn't. There was something in her voice that spoke to the secret, lonely part of him that he'd never been able to share with his parents or sisters; that had always made him feel different from everyone he knew. With the help of his friend, Mercutio, he told her his feelings, and they began to meet in private. The love between them – he doesn't have the words, he hopes Luigi might find them, on his behalf. It felt like there was nothing else that mattered; it made the world feel smaller and bigger all at once. And she felt it too.

But then he was drafted for battle. Giulietta was terrified. 'If you die,' she said, 'I will end my life too. For me this world will not be worth living in without you.'

The young soldier was shivering now so hard it was difficult for him to speak, says Luigi, his own voice dropping a little. Despite the pain, he'd been pressing the bandages against the wound, trying to slow the flow of blood.

'Don't talk if it's too much,' Luigi urged him.

'I need to finish,' he replied.

When Giulietta made this pledge to end her life if he was killed, the young soldier foolishly did not try to dissuade her. In the heat of the moment, it had seemed the most romantic way to say goodbye. But now he *was* going to die, and he knew one thing: he wanted her to live. She was only seventeen years old. She was beautiful; there was a kindness in her, a sixth sense when it came to understanding others, that had seemed unimaginable to him before he met her. For Giulietta to kill herself – and he knew she would do it – would be the worst tragedy of all.

'So what would you have me do?' Luigi asked him, his head full of the beauty of this young man's love, but also of thoughts of his own Lucina.

'Write it,' begged the young man. 'Write down our story so that whatever happens, she may live forever.'

Then he told Luigi his name, Romeo Montecchi, shortly before he lost consciousness.

Luigi looks back up at me, then. His eyes are full of tears, his lashes clumping into little spikes. He sits back in his chair, a little too far away from the microphone for my liking.

'So you see, Vita, that is my confession. The story that I claim is mine, that Shakespeare stole from me, isn't really anything to do with me. If Romeo had lived, Shakespeare would never have written his play at all. (Which, by the way,' he says, lowering his voice, 'needs some editing, don't you agree? The *timing* of it is just not credible.) But I kept my promise. Once I was back at my villa in Montorso Vicentino, and Lucina had made it clear she didn't want to be with me, I began to write.

'I made enquiries first, about a young woman in Vicenza named Giulietta. I wanted to find her before she heard the news of Romeo dying, to tell her his last wish: that she should live her life.'

His voice catches.

'But I was too late. By the time I tracked her down, she'd already done it. Made a sleeping mixture for herself that she knew she would never wake from, and then took herself down to the riverbank and drank it.'

He reaches for a glass of water, and I see his hand is shaking a little.

'I still wonder, if I had found her in time, whether I would have been able to persuade her otherwise. And perhaps if I had, maybe Lucina would have loved me enough to come back. Perhaps she would have seen me as someone who was still useful.'

'Luigi… I… don't know what to say. This is…'

He nods. 'I'm not sure I have much of a "why" for you. But I can tell you this: I'm as bad a liar as I was a lover. I tried to elevate my love life to something more than it was. The truth is a sorry, pedestrian tale. The injured nobleman, a love that was not strong enough. Lucina's love didn't run deep, but in the end, even mine felt confected, second-hand, inspired more by books and ideas than it was by the person herself.

'But once I'd written down the young soldier's tale, something shifted in me. I never stopped missing Lucina, or perhaps the person that I was with her. But I accepted it, I accepted that she had never loved me, and that what I had felt was limited too. And once I did, something in my body changed. The doctors said I'd never walk again. But from that day I began to learn to, with a limp. These days, you can see, I don't do so badly…'

He sighs, raises his hands in the air before dropping them as if to say, *Well, there we go*, and sits back in the chair. He looks flushed, shamed, a little bit relieved.

I feel something rise in me that I haven't ever felt for Luigi. That I didn't want to feel. *Pity*. In the end he didn't really have a love story at all. Not Juliet's. Not even Lucina's.

'So that's my real confession,' he says. 'The source of my pain. Not that I'm the forgotten author of a great love story. Or that I ended up as a footnote in history. But that, by continuing to put myself in someone else's narrative, I was never brave enough to find out who I really was.' He looks up. I see my own sadness mirrored in his eyes.

20

The Wrong Story

Three days and not much sleep later, Danny Cousins emails me back. Just a two-line email telling me that these days he's working full-time in a design company and is happily married with kids (so basically, fuck off) and asking for my address. The next day a package arrives. Inside are three photos and a dog-eared manuscript of *The Verona Diaries*, the screenplay about Luigi and Lucina that I thought I'd lost years ago, with a Post-it note: 'You once told me to burn this!' stuck on the front.

Two of the photos are bad quality, taken in the gloomy light of the church. One shows the portrait of Luigi at his desk with a quill in his hand, wearing the same clothes he turned up in on Day 126. In the other, he is preening in full armour, a battlescape behind him. To the far left, amidst some trees – so peripheral I don't at first notice – is a woman, with long, pale hair and a sad, watchful face, I like to think is Lucina Savorgnan.

The final photo is of me, hair shorter than I remember it, taken outside the ruined shell of the Palladian villa where Luigi became a recluse for seventeen years after he was injured. The same house where, thinking of both Lucina and the young soldier who'd died beside him, he wrote the story that became *Romeo and Juliet*.

Holding the manuscript in my hand after all these years feels strange. It's not that I have a sudden, intuitive flash that it's a work of genius and that all nineteen production companies have missed out on a masterpiece. But something about my glowing expression as I stand in front of the villa makes me think there might be *something* there, some kernel of passion that could be mined and reformed and turned into something good.

That evening, I run myself a bubble bath and read the screenplay with a feeling of ceremony, candlelight flickering across the ceiling. When I reach the last page, I look up at the dancing shadows and laugh for the longest time.

I am still smiling when I walk out the bathroom, wrapped in a towel, and see that a note has been slipped under the door.

My first thought is that it's from Max, who has gone climbing for a few days, to clear his head, he said, and 'so we can both get used to being on our own'. But the handwriting is far too legible, elegant even. As soon as I realise my error, I gallop to the end of the note, then lean back against the arm of the sofa and read it again.

She's hanging in there, it says, *stable enough to be brought home, although in a deep sleep, which no one knows whether she'll come out of. If you'd like to come up and visit her, please do. There's no telling whether she can hear anyone. But being Mrs R., I suspect she probably can. Either way, I have a feeling she would like it – me too.*

J.

'"*Me too*?"' echoes a triumphant voice behind me. 'Well. There we have it.'

Luigi is sitting with his feet crossed on the kitchen table, hands loosely locked behind his head, looking relaxed, buoyant even – a far cry from the broken ghost I'd last seen behind the microphone.

'Uh-uh,' I say, pinning the towel more closely around me, 'don't leap to romantic conclusions.'

'Oh, come *on*,' he says, pushing back his chair and hobbling towards me. 'It's a whopping hint. Let me see.'

I share the piece of paper with him, scowling. I've been longing to see Luigi for the last three days, willing the yellow armchair to manifest him. Once, feeling rather desperate, I even put out a bowl of Twiglets (which, yes, did make me feel a bit childish, like I was leaving out mince pies and carrots for Father Christmas and his reindeers). But now that he is here, I just feel cross and abandoned.

We both look down at the note.

'"*I have a feeling she would like it*", he reads out, "*me too*." I beg your pardon... there's even a dash. A drum roll, if you will, before the key phrase: dash, "me too".'

'Just a kindness,' I mutter. 'To show me there are no hard feelings.'

Luigi smirks. 'On the contrary, *cara*, I think you'll find his feelings are very hard indeed.'

I roll my eyes, although it's an exciting thought. Looking down at the note, I find my thoughts drift to the physical fact of Jesse, only metres away from where I'm standing. He'll be in Mrs R's bedroom, no doubt, maybe playing music to keep her company as she sleeps, alive to the mystery of whatever realm her spirit might be in. *There's no telling whether she can hear anyone.* And then I let myself imagine him lying across the end of my bed, cheek cupped in one hand, looking at me with those smiling eyes, at ease with the stagnant boredom of the sickroom. Not trying to fix me, or escape. Content just to be there with me *except*... I blink away the vision, feel again the awful jolt as Jesse pushes me away on the landing, remembering the landslide of humiliation in my chest. *There I go again*, I realise with a kind of amused horror, *this is what I always do.* I lurch into the idea of love as a way out. What was it that Luigi said? *I was never brave enough to find out who I really was.*

'No way,' I say, starting back up the stairs to the mezzanine. 'I'm not going up there. Not yet. Not while she's unconscious.'

I hear Luigi's uneven step behind me.

'Isn't that a bit of a gamble, *amore mio?*'

I shake my head, keep walking.

'Because wouldn't it be terrible,' he persists, between breaths, 'if you were too late again?'

Too late again.

I spin around at this, suddenly furious.

'Screw you, Luigi.' I glare at him. 'Screw you and your misplaced meddling.'

He puts up both hands quickly. 'Forgive me, *bella*! *Per favore.* I overstepped. I know you really care about Mrs Rothwell. That's all that matters now. Which is why I can't help thinking…' He hesitates.

I look at him suspiciously. 'Well?'

He spreads his hands. 'The photo.'

I want to retort, '*What photo?*' Except I've reached the top step now and I'm staring straight at it. The stolen photo of the Rothwells in the park, young and in love. The one that set off the argument between me and Max in the first place. Which I'd not put back in the drawer after he left, but kept on the bedside table, angled towards me. As a reminder, when the doubts came, about the difference: the gap between love as a story we tell ourselves, and love as something true.

'It should be on her bedside table,' says Luigi, as he takes a seat in the yellow armchair. 'It could be what she needs to wake up to. Wouldn't it be dreadful if—'

'*Luigi!* Stop stirring the pot.'

He shrugs and looks away, eyebrows arched. 'I'm simply here to tell you what you already know.'

I close my eyes. He's right, of course. It could happen any time. I have to take it upstairs. The fact that it means facing Jesse should not stop me doing what's right.

Taking a deep breath, I walk over to my chest of drawers to pull out some underwear. The full-length mirror propped in the corner has been angled away for as long as I can remember, but I tilt it round now as I drop the towel to get dressed. The sight of my naked body stops me for a moment.

I am a little skinnier than before I got sick, it's true. My arse is a little flatter, my boobs a touch smaller. But it's not a disaster. In fact, with the light falling across my stomach, leaving pools of shadow along the curve of my hip bone and between my thighs…

I glance up to see Luigi is looking at me, too.

'Do you mind?' I say sharply.

He shrugs, lifts both hands in surprise. 'Not at all. Why? Do you?'

I think for a moment. 'Not especially, I suppose.'

'That's good.' He smiles; devilish, admiring. 'Because you really shouldn't.'

I carry on getting dressed.

21

The Last Gasp

It takes me twenty minutes to lug Whitney Houston down from the mezzanine and then up to Mrs Rothwell's flat. Luigi, it turns out, is a fat lot of help, though he does take my mind off the butterflies in my stomach and the ache in my arms by rambling on about his episode of *Confessions* – which, now that he's had a chance to reflect on it, *was* kind of a masterpiece, and had I any thoughts on how to achieve maximum impact? Because he, Luigi, was pretty fed up with centuries of being an unsung genius, and without wanting to lecture me about my job, everyone knew that these days marketing was all about social media.

'No rush,' he says impatiently, as I lean panting against the wall, the water sloshing about the bowl.

As soon as we reach Mrs Rothwell's door the nerves come flooding back. I feel the photo frame that's digging into my arse through the back pocket of my jeans and my heart speeds up.

'Over to you,' murmurs Luigi, taking a step back into the shadows.

'*Stop!* Why?' I hiss back angrily. 'Why do you always disappear at the difficult moments?'

'Because you don't actually need me,' he replies, *sotto voce,* just as the door opens.

Jesse looks tired; bloodshot eyes, unshaven, and even more attractive than I remembered. His gaze drops to the fishbowl I'm holding in both arms.

'Well, that's impressive,' he says.

'I thought Mrs R might like some company,' I say, my ears burning. 'Best sickbed companion in the business.'

I hover by Mrs Rothwell's bedroom door as Jesse walks in with Whitney Houston and carefully places the bowl on the bedside table.

It's a shock seeing how old and frail she looks. Since the ambulance took her away, I've found myself replaying certain moments during my visits upstairs. A few seconds here or there, as she stood up from her chair, or leaned back after a heavy bout of laughter, when the life-force she emanated seemed to dim or flicker. But this is of a different order, like someone has ripped out the plug at the mains.

Jesse must have propped her up, folding the sheet down under her hands so that she looks like she has tucked herself in elegantly for an afternoon's nap. But her face is gaunt, her breathing is laboured, and her mouth slightly parted so that I can see a crust of dried white spit on her lips. And she looks much smaller than I remembered, like her body has begun to withdraw from the space it takes up in the world.

I hear Max's voice in my head: *They're really sick.* This, then, is what he meant – the kind of sickness that means life or death – and all at once I'm back in the tumble dryer of self-doubt and self-disgust and I wonder if I've made a huge mistake, demonising Max and his straight lines and certainties. Though looking at Mrs Rothwell, her face turning into a skull before me, why does any of it matter if such a vibrant life force can be so instantly and utterly reduced?

Jesse glances back at me but doesn't comment on my expression.

'I'll leave you two for a moment,' he says. 'You know how long that weird coffee machine of hers takes.'

As soon as he has gone, the silence takes on a different quality.

I walk over and sit on the chair by her bed. Up close, her breathing is even more ragged. Someone has filed her nails into perfect crescent moons but her fingers resting on the sheet are slack. I thought that I had a lot to say; that it would all come spilling out as soon as I was at her bedside. But my mind blanks completely.

I look over at the fishbowl where the coloured gravel is drifting back slowly to settle on the bottom. Whitney stares back at me, letting out a stream of bubbles.

'She may not look like the sharpest tool in the box, but I've found her a great source of wisdom.'

My voice sounds awkward in the empty room. No, not empty, I think. Mrs Rothwell is still here.

'Not sure about you but I find the hardest part about being sick is you've no idea when it will end.'

More silence.

'I mean, if someone could give you a *date*, an exact time and date when you'll be released, I think you could bear just about anything. It's the not-knowing that drives you mad. But Whitney doesn't worry about that. She's just happy going round in circles.'

The spit rattles in Mrs Rothwell's throat. I look away, feeling idiotic, and imagine Luigi leaning in the corner, arms crossed, raising a sceptical eyebrow. *That's really all you've got,* cara mia*?*

But what the hell am I supposed to say? I squeeze Mrs Rothwell's hand as I think.

'I lied about having known Maya.' I wait as if for a response, for the shock and betrayal to wake Mrs R from her sleep, but nothing. 'I never met her or knew her. The scene at the speeding course was a lie. Lifted right from a story my sister once told me about herself.' The silence begins to feel inviting.

'It was a split-second reflex. I saw a chance to stop you feeling… not the loss, but some of the guilt and regret that was haunting you. The fact that she died when the two of you were on bad terms. I know all about that and I thought I could, in some small way, soften it. You said it was like I brought Maya back into the room. I wanted to do the same for my sister, Gracie. She's dead also; six months ago, from an epileptic fit. I wanted her back in the room, too.' I break off, feel a painful constriction in my chest. 'Like you and Maya, we argued a lot, mostly about things she wanted to talk about and I wanted to leave unsaid.'

I am caught again by the memory of that day in Brighton, walking back into Gracie's flat after having stormed out towards the station, thankful at least that I'd turned round, back for that muddled truce and her tickling my arm just up to the mole in the crook of my elbow. I close my eyes, tip-toe my fingers up my arm. *Say when.* What about never, Gracie? If I didn't say 'when', would you still be here, beside me?

'I tried to make you feel that there was no anger in Maya's heart towards you when she died, because that's what I desperately wanted to feel about Gracie. Because I have no idea how she felt about me when she died, if she was still hurt or disappointed, or both. It haunted me, not knowing. I guess I thought that at least I could prevent that, for you.' I drag my teeth across my lower lip. 'It was selfish and wrong. I won't ask you to forgive me, just to know why I did it.' Mrs Rothwell's breathing is heavy, but regular and reassuring. 'For what it's worth, I now see that we both had complicated love affairs. What I had with my sister is something that outlives death and time. She's gone but she's also here. I hope sometimes you can feel that too.'

I sit looking at her hand in mine. I so want her to wake up, to tell her she's got more living to do, to thank her for the way my life began to change the minute her world started flooding into mine, for everything that she inspired.

The sound of mugs clinking in the kitchen. Jesse would be back soon. I stand up quickly and pull the small frame out of my back pocket.

'Really sorry I nicked this,' I say, trying to find some room to prop it just behind the fishbowl. So that if she opens her eyes she'll see it, but without Jesse clocking its sudden appearance. 'I think I wanted to understand what you two had. *Have*.'

More raspy breathing.

I fiddle a bit more with the angle of the photo, move it closer, a couple more centimetres, but then all of a sudden my elbow is pushing Whitney's bowl further out and then… fuck, fuck… *crash!*

Whitney Houston is flopping about on the floor amidst shards of glass and scattered rainbow gravel. It's like a riddle or a metaphor or something, except it's not. It's happening in real life, now, and I'm not imagining it. Neither am I imagining the fact that Mrs Rothwell still has not stirred, and I'm rooted to the spot rather than diving to the rescue. I'm standing there, frozen, as my goldfish spasms on the carpet, thinking, *She's going to die, she's going to die, and it's all my fault*. And then it's not the fish I'm seeing at all, it's Gracie, lying on a tiled floor, her body jerking, and I can't move, I can't move…

'What the hell? Oh, *shit*.'

Jesse is down on the floor right away, scooping with his palms to try and grab Whitney as she flaps about in panic, and saying, *Pass the water glass,* and finally I wake up and grab the tumbler from the bedside table and somehow he's flicked her up from the carpet, and she's in.

We stare down into the glass.

Whitney Houston doesn't move. Her tail is curled to one side, her mouth agape.

'She needs more room. I'll run the bath,' yells Jesse, sprinting towards the bathroom.

I run after him, using my hand to cup the top of the glass in case I spill her out. He's putting the plug in and spinning the taps and we're both standing staring grim-faced at the tub, willing it to fill up faster. The side panel is still off from the day that it flooded, showing the bottom of the bath and all its dusty pipes, and for a moment I imagine myself lying in the bedroom below, pale-faced and vacant as the watermarks spread.

'Okay now… careful…'

I tip the glass until it is a couple of inches from the water. Whitney Houston lands with a soft *plop*.

Jesse turns the taps off, and we both stare down anxiously into the tub. There is an agonising moment as she seems to drift around, though you can't tell what's moving, her or the current. Then she bobs up and comes to rest on her side on the surface, glassy eye blank and unmoving.

Jesse puts his hand on my arm.

'Sorry, Vita.'

I nod dumbly, my throat tight.

Not again. Please, not again.

Just as I turn away, unable to bear it, her tail twitches, then flicks from one side to the other, and suddenly she is zooming around the bathtub and Jesse and I are whooping with relief.

'Oh, thank God.' My chest is so full I have to sit down on the edge of the bath. Jesse sits down next to me. I'm trembling so hard my legs are jiggling against the side of the tub.

'I'm sorry,' I say, laughing so as not to cry, as he puts out a hand to steady me. 'I feel like I…' I see myself stealing the photo; putting it back; holding forth about Maya '… keep doing the wrong things for the right reasons.'

I have a flash of myself leaning towards him as I did on the landing, the roughness of his stubble, the salty taste of his mouth, and suddenly the bathroom shrinks into a tiny space around us. I dig my nails in my palms until they hurt. Don't forget what he said: *I'm not your way out.*

Jesse is looking down at Whitney Houston as she circles the bath lazily. Part of the collar of his denim shirt is sticking up at a weird angle. I want to fix it for him, smooth it down.

'Do you think she'll be okay?' he asks. And before I can say something flip, about the bath being a pretty good upgrade, he adds, his voice catching, 'Mrs R, I mean.'

We both sit in silence for a moment.

'It's the hardest part,' I say, after a while. 'I just think, there's no knowing.'

He looks up at me then. Eyes very steady, not smiling, but looking straight into me.

'You're right,' he says, holding my gaze. 'There's no knowing.'

And it feels like he is saying out loud: *Or perhaps we do know.*

His hand is very close to mine on the edge of the bath.

I stand up. 'I better go downstairs.'

A flicker of surprise, perhaps even disappointment, crosses Jesse's face. 'Already? You sure?'

All at once the flat feels like a refuge. I want to be back in my bed, even if that means staring up at the ceiling again.

'Yes,' I say, and it sounds like a decision, 'I am.' I look down at the tub. 'Not sure how to get Whitney Houston back downstairs, though.'

He stands up too, putting his hands in his pockets. 'Why don't you leave her with me for a while?'

I hesitate for a moment. 'Good idea.' Then I lean down over the bath as Whitney swings round again. 'Don't forget me,' I whisper to my goldfish.

Jesse grins, looking at the fish, then up at me. 'How could she?'

Jesse walks me out. 'Do you want some help cleaning up the mess?' I ask. 'There's broken glass and fish furniture everywhere.' He shakes his head. No need, he tells me, it's nice to be useful. As we walk past Mrs Rothwell's room I glimpse her unmoving on the pillow, in the strange, deep sleep she's in. I think about all the months I've been like that, too, dead to the world, with people walking down the street outside my window.

The living, passing by the invisible sick. Every day, everywhere. Because that's what we all do.

22

Day 163

I've never been any good at packing, I procrastinate too much. Gracie would say I have a problem with facing endings, and there is that. But I think she'd agree that over the last few days, even if it's slowly, I'm doing better on that front.

The day after Max left to go climbing, I discovered we still had the flattened boxes from when I moved in six months ago. This came as a surprise to me, but then again, I wasn't exactly all there, only two weeks after being told that Gracie had cracked her head in the shower during a fit. According to the coroner she died around 9 a.m., just about the time I was standing under my own shower in a different apartment, deliberating whether to call and tell her that the answer to five down was 'fragment', and that, by the way, I loved her more than anything in the world and I was sorry, so fucking sorry, that I'd been too young to understand how to protect her. (Would I have said that bit? Probably not. But I like to think, maybe.)

At some point every day, I try to face the fact Gracie has died. That we'll never watch another movie together and argue over the ending, or compete over crossword clues, and bitch about Faye. That she won't go diving with me in Cornwall again, and lie about her epilepsy when filling out forms, because she's fucked if it will cheat her out of a single experience more than it already has.

I turn my mind to it, and I feel it.

Although it doesn't change much physically, mentally The Pit is easier to cope with these days. I no longer feel that I am at war with my mind. That I have chopped it off from the rest of my body, as Mrs Rothwell once put it. But there are downsides, too. Before, even through all the pain, I could summon the past and those moments with Gracie with a peculiar clarity. One of the flipsides of an illness that destabilises reality is that you get to time-travel. While you are stuck, nothing is in the past.

This morning, after taping up the last of four boxes (I'm surprised at how little I have, the flat doesn't look so different once I'm done), I decide to write a letter to Max. I've been composing it in my head ever since our fight, so it should have written itself by this point. But when I sit down at the kitchen table with a sheet of paper from the printer, I find myself writing to someone else instead.

Dear Mrs Rothwell,

I hope Jesse is reading this to you. Don't worry, it's not another confession. This time I think you'll approve: I'm moving out. Of my flat, but also my situation with Max. I'm not sure where I'm going yet. Or what I'll be doing for a living. Only that it's going to be something different. When I'm back up and running, I'm going to quit the podcast too. Jesse was right when he basically told me it was a phoney piece of junk. Annoyingly, it turns out he is right about a lot of things.

But I'll come and visit, if I may, from time to time. And in the meantime, I hope you'll let Whitney Houston stay on for a while. I know she couldn't think of anywhere she'd rather be.

With love and thanks,

Vita

P.S. Please look out for Max. He could do with some custard tart and daytime TV. Then again, I recommend you tap him up to do a refurb on all the common parts in the house. Quite apart from the dodgy plumbing in the building, the stairwell carpet is in a dire way. Don't feel bad about squeezing him for cash. He's about to make a ton of money telling rich neurotics how to live longer based on the state of their shit. Also don't let Jesse take the tenner off you. It's not that I'm too good for Max. It's just that I'd like to be better at being on my own.

I seal the envelope. Then, after a glance at the boxes that are sitting stacked in the hall, I begin to climb the stairs to drop off my letter.

I am feeling so full of purpose that it's a shocking disappointment to feel the symptoms creep in on the third step. My fingers and toes start to fizz and then lose feeling and my vision begins to swim, so I sit down and do some breathing. 'You're just nervous,' says Luigi's voice. Looking around, I see he's sitting a couple of steps above me, looking down his nose with legs elegantly crossed. 'Stress and fear, as well as too much activity, is going to affect your nervous system for a while.' He goes on to explain how there are two ways to look at these hovering symptoms. Either I can feel forever unsafe, ready to slip back any moment, arms wheeling, into The Pit. Or I can see them as a kind of superpower, warning me about the things that other people ignore, spooking me just enough to listen to my body and mind more vigilantly. To watch out ducking the anger and grief, for becoming a version of myself that I think other people want.

He examines his nails, his voice turning casual.

'By the way, any second thoughts about the script?'

I shake my head. 'I'm sorry. But it really is as big a pile of shit as they said it was.'

'Not even—'

'Irretrievably shit. Sorry. But I've been thinking about what to do with your *Confessions*. In fact, I've got a bit of an idea...' I flex my fingers in the air, moving them over an imaginary keyboard.

Looking intrigued, Luigi stands up and proffers his arm. 'Are we going upstairs now? I promised you I'd stay with you all the way, didn't I?'

Walking the rest of the stairs is much easier on his arm. I feel my pulse-rate slow. The sticky sludge in my veins starts to move, like warm water sputtering through frozen pipes. By the time I reach Mrs Rothwell's door, everything feels possible again.

I make a fist to knock, remarking to Luigi about the hall light, which seems to have stopped doing its blackout intervals. When he doesn't answer, I look around.

'Luigi?' I call out along the empty hallway, and then back down the stairs. '*Luigi?*'

But the silence feels different, and I realise he's gone again. Perhaps I'm being over-dramatic, but somehow I get the feeling he's not coming back.

I lower my fist, still looking down the hallway. The sun is pouring in through the fanlight above the front door where I can see the peeling stencil of the number 43, written backwards. I hesitate for a moment, undecided. Then I slip the letter in the pocket of my trousers. I can always give it to Jesse after I go for a walk.

The front door is heavier than I remembered. The leaves on the copper beech tree across the street are turning the same shade as my sister's hair when she was a girl.

I take a step outside, feel the sharpness of the cool air as I draw it up through my nostrils and down into my lungs, and I start walking.

AUTHOR'S NOTE

Luigi da Porto was born 1485 in Vicenza and died forty-four years later. He is a mostly forgotten writer whose novella – *Newly Found Story of Two Nobles* – tells the tale of Romeo Montague and Juliet Capulet.

The oil paintings I describe in the church in Verona do not exist. The dying soldier who inspires Luigi da Porto is also pure invention.

The inspiration for the novella is disputed. In 1511, Luigi apparently fell in love with his cousin Lucina Savorgnan, after seeing her sing at a ball. The lovers then met in secret. But the two arms of their family were at war. Lucina was betrothed to another, and a few months later, Luigi was paralysed by a spear wound in the Battle of Friuli. He became a recluse, living out his days in the country villa where he wrote the novella. He dedicated it to Lucina.

Over sixty years after it was published, William Shakespeare wrote *Romeo and Juliet*.

ACKNOWLEDGEMENTS

As soon as I was well enough to write, it felt like this book fell out of my head: It didn't. Thank you to all who helped me along the tricky and sometimes painful path of writing fiction based on a real illness: my agent Claire Conrad (who put the idea of writing a shorter novel in my head); my brilliant editors Alexis Kirschbaum, Allegra Le Fanu and all the team at Bloomsbury including Helen Upton for spreading the word, Faye Robinson and Lynn Curtis for their meticulous eye for detail, and Greg Heinimann for another stunning cover. In the US, the excellent Gaby Mongelli and Marya Spence as well as Sally Kim, Tarini Sipahimalani and everyone involved at Putnam Penguin: thank you for your diligence, enthusiasm and vision.

I'm also wildly lucky to have a bunch of talented readers closer to home: Leo Carey, Ellie and Alex Simon, Lucinda Vaughan, Charlotte Edwardes, Emma Hewitt, Carey Mackenzie and my magical (and ass-kicking) sisters, Joanna, Sam and Zumbs. Thank you for your time, generosity and insight. Huge thanks also to Richard Rogan for letting me channel his crossword brain and Jon Hill for his design genius.

Thank you to Dr Michael Harding and Dr Iona Cobb, who went beyond the black-and-white thinking that so many of those with invisible illnesses, including myself, have experienced in medical hands. Thank you to Lauren Stoney for awakening me to the neural traps tangled up in physical illnesses. To all my friends who held my hand, especially Sasha Filskow: you'll never know how much you helped me.

Above all, thanks to my children Samuel and Elsie, for the endless cups of tea they brought me in bed, their patience and pride in my writing, for Samuel's brilliant views on titles and covers, and Elsie's terrifyingly sharp eye for close edits. My love and admiration for you goes beyond words.

It's hard to know who is more difficult to live with, a sick person or a writer. Thank you, James for doing both. For your love, brilliance, and insight, in writing as in life. For listening out for the gap between the words and the feeling. And for making it seem – fifteen years in – that the adventure has just begun.